COUNTDOWN TO DISASTER

DATE: April 14, 1912
PLACE: R.M.S. *Titanic*, somewhere in the North Atlantic

- 11P.M. First Wireless Operator John Phillips, attempting to get a backlog of outgoing messages out through his hookup with *Cape Race.* is interrupted by another, more frantic message from the *Californian* which, at this time, is between 10 and 19 miles north of the *Titanic*. The message is: "I say, old man, we're stopped and surrounded by ice." Before the *Californian* can give its coordinates, an irritated Phillips shouts back, "Shut up! Shut up! I'm busy! I'm working *Cape Race!*" and cuts off the *Californian*'s message.

- 11:30 P.M. The *Titanic* is proceeding along at crusing speed of $22^1/2$ knots, moving at a rate of 38 feet per second.

- 11:40 P.M. Lookout Fleet spots an iceberg approximately 500 yards ahead. Its height is approximately 60 feet. He clangs the crow's nest bell three times and immediately gets on the phone with a three-word message: "Iceberg right ahead!"

The Byron Preiss Multimedia
Worldwide Website address is:
http//www.byronpreiss.com

The Total Titanic Worldwide Website address is:
http//www.totaltitanic.com

For Orders other than by individual consumers, Pocket Books grants a discount on the purchase of 10 or more copies of single titles for special markets or premium use. For further details, please write to the Vice-President of Special Markets, Pocket Books, 1633 Broadway, New York, NY 10019-6785 8th Floor.

For information on how individual consumers can place orders, please write to Mail Order Department, Simon & Schuster, Inc., 200 Old Tappan Road, Old Tappan, NJ 07675.

TOTAL TITANIC

THE MOST UP-TO-DATE GUIDE
TO THE DISASTER OF THE CENTURY

Marc Shapiro

BYRON PREISS MULTIMEDIA COMPANY, INC.
NEW YORK

POCKET BOOKS
NEW YORK LONDON TORONTO SYDNEY TOKYO SINGAPORE

An *Original* Publication of POCKET BOOKS

POCKET BOOKS, a division of Simon & Schuster Inc.
1230 Avenue of the Americas, New York, NY 10020

Byron Preiss Multimedia Company, Inc.
24 West 25th Street
New York, New York 10010

The Byron Preiss Multimedia Worldwide Web Site address is:
http://www.byronpreiss.com

ISBN 0-671-01202-9

First Pocket Books paperback printing March 1998

10 9 8 7 6 5 4 3 2 1

Edited by Ruth Ashby and Howard Zimmerman
Cover design by Arnie Sawyer Studio
Interior design by MM Design 2000, Inc.

Printed in the U.S.A.

To
Nancy and Rachael

CONTENTS

INTRODUCTION

The R.M.S. *Titanic* struck an iceberg in the North Atlantic at 11:40 P.M. on April 14, 1912. By 2:20 A.M. on April 15, the last visible section of the *Titanic* sank below the icy ocean waters. More than 1,500 passengers and crew lost their lives. Only some 700 people survived.

It has been called greatest sea tragedy of all time. In the wake of the disaster, the *Titanic* and the events surrounding its ill-fated journey have become part of twentieth-century myth, giving rise to numerous books, movies and, more recently, World Wide Web sites. As with all great mysteries, much that has been written and said about the event either stretches the truth or disregards it entirely. Only two of the following three widely circulated pieces of *Titanic* lore, for instance, are accurate. One is untrue, but continues to exist as part of the legend.

What is fact and what is fiction?

• In 1898, American author Morgan Robertson published a novel called *Futility* in which a British ocean liner, on its maiden voyage, strikes an iceberg and

1

sinks. This fictional voyage took place in April. The collision took place in the North Atlantic. The liner was named the *Titan*.

• The *Titanic* was originally scheduled to make its maiden voyage on March 20, 1912. The date was changed to April 10 after the *Titanic*'s sister ship, the *Olympic*, collided with the British Navy cruiser *Hawke* while under the command of Captain Edward J. Smith, the future captain of the *Titanic*.

• The last song played by the band aboard the *Titanic* as it went down was "Nearer My God To Thee."

Fact is often stranger than fiction, so it should come as no surprise that the story about Robertson's novel is devastatingly accurate, no matter how far-fetched. So is the report of Captain Smith's collision with the naval cruiser. However, as logical and poetically ironic as it would have been for the band to have played "Nearer My God To Thee" as the ship sank, this story is not true. The band is reported to have played "Songe d'Autumne" for its final performance.

Total Titanic will separate fiction from fact and report on what actually happened as best we know it, from personal memoirs, official records, and discoveries made on recent expeditions to the ship's ocean-bottom grave site. In addition, you will find a treasure trove of information about the fictional versions of the tragedy, from the classic novel-turned-into-film *A*

Night to Remember to the 1997 James Cameron box office blockbuster.

For the aficionado, there is also a full passenger and crew manifest, an important element of the *Titanic*'s legacy. It should be remembered that these were real people whose lives were cut short by accident, ignorance, and catastrophe. But their story lives on. It is now part of our cultural heritage, and their names will not be forgotten.

Here, now, are the true and untainted facts about the sailing—and sinking—of the R.M.S. *Titanic*.

CHAPTER 1

THE MAKING OF THE *TITANIC*

In 1912, the world was poised on the precipice of change. Behind it lay the Victorian Age, an era of optimistic belief in the inevitability of progress and of unprecedented strides in science, technology, and industry. Before it lay the deadly and disillusioning no-man's-land of World War I. By the time the war was over, the comfortable assumptions of prewar Europe had been shattered.

But all that lay in the future, and in the present there was money to be made and fun to be had. In 1912, what Mark Twin had dubbed the Gilded Age was still in full ostentatious swing. The growth of industry had spawned a new generation of wealth on both sides of the Atlantic: In 1861, there were only three millionaires in the United States; by 1900, there were 3,800 of them. Fortunes were made and lost and made again. Those who had money wanted to spend it: on bigger and more opulent homes, on clothes and furnishings and travel and yachts. Nothing was too grand, nothing too elaborate, for the new moneyed classes of Europe and the United States.

5

And right in the middle of it was the White Star Line, preparing to take the next big step.

The British-based White Star Line had gone through a number of changes since its formation in 1850. Initially a goods and services outfit, plying its trade in the Australian goldfields, the company had turned its attention to oceangoing passenger steamships when purchased by Thomas Henry Ismay in 1867. Ismay's first ship, the *Oceanic*, completed by the Belfast ship-building firm of Harland and Wolff in 1871, introduced innovations, like promenade decks, that greatly increased passenger comfort and became the rule on subsequent liners.

When Thomas Henry Ismay died in 1899, his 38-year-old son, J. Bruce Ismay, took over the company. J. Bruce Ismay had a real sense of both business and style. He loved the good things in life and was willing to do whatever was necessary to make a profit. Together with Lord W. J. Pirrie, the chairman of Harland and Wolff, he considered a proposal by American financial wizard J. P. Morgan to buy White Star Line as part of a scheme to unite all Atlantic shipping lines in one trust. In 1902, Morgan purchased the White Star Line for his International Mercantile Marine and installed J. Bruce Ismay as the company's president in 1904.

The White Star Line was a utopian concept under the Morgan banner. Although the company was essentially American, with controlling American interests, the ships of the White Star Line were very much a British operation in tone and execution. (It was agreed that in time of war, its ships could be appropriated by the British navy.) The White Star Line continued to prosper with its existing line of ships. But, as always, its owners were looking to the future and to bigger and better things.

History-making decisions were now only a few years away.

At a 1907 dinner party, J. Bruce Ismay proposed the construction of two luxury-class ocean liners, to be known as the Olympic class, to go head to head with the Cunard Line for the lucrative Atlantic passenger trade. A third ship was added to the proposal at a later date.

There was good reason to begin thinking of making economic war against Cunard. For years White Star and Cunard had competed for the booming passenger market, and both had seemed satisfied with their fair share. But new steamship companies from Europe had entered the race, and Cunard had decided that, to surpass the competition, they needed to upgrade their line. They built the *Lusitania* and the *Mauretania*—the biggest, fastest ships on the North Atlantic route. That they could carry more passengers than anything currently under the White Star banner was almost beside the point. The real problem was that Cunard would now be the premier steamship company in the world—and that White Star would be in second place.

In July 1908, Ismay and Morgan signed a contract with Harland and Wolff for the construction of the three luxury liners. The early specs indicate ships 50 percent larger than the *Lusitania*'s 30,000 gross tons and an estimated 100 feet longer than its 790 feet. These liners would be the true gods of the sea. They would be named *Olympic*, *Titanic,* and *Britannic*.

• J. Bruce Ismay and designer Thomas Andrews's plan for the *Titanic* was as follows:

> Passenger and crew capacity: 3,547.
> Weight: 46,328 tons.
> Length: 882 feet, 9 inches.
> Width: 94 feet.
> Height: 100 feet at bridge level.
> Water displacement: 66,000 tons.
> Watertight doors: 42 (12 of which can be opened and closed from the bridge).

• The *Titanic* design included 29 boilers, 159 furnaces, and funnels which were situated 73 feet above the boat deck. The *Titanic*'s estimated speed included 46,000 horsepower capacity and is estimated to be capable of 24 knots at full speed.

• Total cost: 1,500,000 pounds ($7,500,000 US).

• Each of the ship's funnels was large enough to drive two trains through.

• The *Titanic* contained a total of nine decks.

• The ship was as tall as an 11-story building.

• The *Titanic*'s three anchors weighed a total of 31 tons. Each link in the anchor chain weighed 175 pounds.

• The ship's rudder weighed 20,250 pounds. The *Titanic* had three propellers; the middle one was 16 feet across, the outer two were 23 feet across.

• The *Titanic*'s boilers weighed 100 tons each.

• The ship contained a total of four elevators, three in first class and one in second class. The *Titanic* was the first boat to have an elevator in second class.

• The *Titanic* design called for 20 lifeboats, 16 wooden and 4 collapsible. This was 10 percent more than was required by the British Board of Trade regulations, which only required lifeboats for 962 people. The designer of the lifeboat davits, Alexander Carlisle, suggested davits capable of carrying more boats. His suggestion was ignored.

• The construction of specially designed slips, capable of holding the *Titanic* and her monster sisters, began on July 31, 1908, on both sides of the Atlantic. A new gantry for the building of the luxury liners also began construction on that date.

• 14,000 workers were hired in preparation for beginning construction on the *Titanic*. They were paid a total of 2 pounds for a 49-hour work week.

- The *Titanic*'s keel was laid down in the Harland and Wolff shipyards on March 31, 1909. The *Titanic* was issued its official number, 401, by the shipbuilders. Its official Board of Trade number was 131,428. External construction on the *Titanic* began that day.

- The *Titanic*'s hull contained three million rivets. Thomas Andrews claimed that together weighed an estimated 1,200 tons.

- The *Titanic*'s hull was successfully launched on May 31, 1911, in front of more than 100,000 people from slip #3 of the Harland and Wolff shipyards. Three tons of soft soap, 15 tons of tallow, and 5 tons of tallow mixed with train oil were used to grease the slipway for the *Titanic* hull.

- The pressure on the hull that day was three tons per square inch.

- Three sets of flags were flying on the day the *Titanic* slid into the ocean for the first time. They were the British Red Ensign, the Stars and Stripes, and a series of navy signal flags that spelled out the message "Good Luck" to mark the occasion.

- The official launch time for *Titanic*'s ceremonial first contact with water was 12:15:02 P.M. The hull was immediately towed to a fitting-out area in another section of the shipyards, where internal construction on the *Titanic* began.

CHAPTER 2

THE ULTIMATE LUXURY LINER

The White Star Line made no bones about who they wanted walking the decks of their proud, new vessel. They wanted the Astors, Guggenheims, and Morgans of the world. They wanted people with money who would spend it freely, have the experience of a lifetime, and most importantly, tell their friends to come along with them on the next voyage.

The *Titanic*'s sister ship, the *Olympic*, was actually the first of the new liners to put to sea, making her maiden voyage on the same day that the *Titanic* was launched, May 3, 1911. His observations of the *Olympic* led J. Bruce Ismay to make numerous changes on the *Titanic* that led to its being truly larger and more luxurious than the *Olympic*; the *Titanic* could even accommodate 163 more passengers. As a result, when it was completed, the *Titanic* was the biggest ship in the world, a floating palace.

The *Titanic* was intended to be something remarkable, and remarkable she was. During the ten months it took to outfit the ship, a good bit of attention was paid to the trappings of finery—with some spectacular results.

Ismay, who regularly had J. P. Morgan's ear, would constantly talk up the idea of elegance. Why not gold ornamentation? he would ask. Why not exquisite statuary? Anybody could lay down just any old rug in the grand saloon. Ismay, with his American partner's blessing and deep pockets, would lay down an oriental rug that was so rich and fine it would make passengers feel as if they were sinking up to their knees in plush.

One of White Star Line's master strokes was the reconfiguring of first-class accommodations on B Deck. With a minimal amount of restructuring, a series of 28 lavish staterooms was installed. Rather than being fitted with traditional portholes, these rooms featured full-sized windows that gave the occupant a seaside view. Each of the rooms reflected one of the many popular architectural styles of the day; passengers could cross the Atlantic in bedrooms decorated in Elizabethan, Louis XVI, Early Dutch, or Regency period furnishings.

When she was finished, the *Titanic* was a glittering reflection of the class-conscious nature of society in 1912. As expected, first-class passengers had the most fabulous accommodations ever seen on board ship. But those traveling second and third class on the *Titanic*'s maiden voyage were treated to a real surprise. Secondclass voyagers had living and dining areas that were the equivalent of first-class conditions on other ships. And third-class passengers, usually emigrants and traditionally given little consideration on their voyage to a new world, found commodious space and ample and wholesome food.

You see, Ismay had a theory that second- and third-class passengers might, someday, be first-class passengers. So he wanted them to have some pleasant memories to draw them back.

• The *Titanic* was the first ocean liner to have a swimming pool and a gymnasium. The swimming pool was situated on F Deck and was open to first-class passengers only. The gymnasium, situated on the starboard side of the ship, featured high arched windows and top-of-the-line exercise equipment, including rowing machines and exercycles.

• The ship contained both Turkish and electric baths, a fully outfitted darkroom for photographers, and a kennel for first-class dogs.

• First-class accommodations included four parlor suites, approximately 50 feet in length and adorned with ornate gold decorations and finely woven rugs. Each contained two bedrooms, a sitting room, and a private bath and lavatory. Two of the four parlor suites had their own private promenade decks.

• The extravagant first-class passenger level also contained a smoking room and a trio of fine dining establishments. The A la Carte Restaurant offered luxury dining and architecture that featured modern leaded windows and very trendy Jacobean-style alcoves. The Veranda Café, also known as the Palm Court, consisted of two dining rooms located on either side of the ship. It featured *Titanic*'s trademark high arched windows, white wicker furniture, and ivy crawling along trellis-covered walls. The Café Parisien, which featured real French chefs and waitresses, was modeled after the famous sidewalk cafés of Paris.

• The first-class lounge was modeled after the famous Palace of Versailles. On the mantlepiece of one of the lounge's fireplaces was a miniature statue of Versailles's Artemis.

• A showcase of first-class luxury was the Grand Staircase, an imposing gathering place enclosed in a glass and wrought-iron skylight. A highlight of any walk upon the Grand Staircase was an elegantly designed clock on the first landing that was flanked by two sculpted figures representing Honor and Glory.

• There were barbershops for every class of passenger.

• Second-class rooms were large and spacious, offering comfortable beds and soothing sycamore paneling on the walls. A second-class dining saloon offered comfortable seating with food cooked in the same kitchen where first-class food was cooked. The second-class smoking room, paneled in heavy oak, was a nightly meeting room for convivial male passengers.

- Third-class single male and female passengers were situated at opposite ends of the ship. The two rooms of the third-class dining saloon were separated by a watertight bulkhead and lined with simple enameled paneling.

- The ship offered an onboard 50-telephone switchboard.

- It had an up-to-date hospital, complete with an operating room.

- The *Titanic*'s modern kitchen contained electric freezers, ovens, and the latest in slicing, peeling, and mincing machines.

CHAPTER 3

THE SAILING OF THE *TITANIC*

*W*hen the *Titanic* emerged from ten months of extensive outfitting and decoration, it was a glittering reflection of the age and the concept of luxury. The Ismay and Morgan clans were thrilled at what they perceived to be the jewel of the newly defined White Star Line and were quick to announce that the maiden voyage of the *Titanic* would be on March 20, 1912.

It would be a classic first voyage. There would be a massive amount of fanfare as the *Titanic*, blessed with an elite passenger list representing the highest levels of material and creative success, steamed out of Southampton, England. Quick stops at Cherbourg, France and Queenstown, Ireland would allow the *Titanic* and its crew the opportunity to get their sea legs before making for the open waters of the North Atlantic en route to the massive celebration that was planned in New York when the jewel of the White Star Line pulled into the dock of its American-based company.

Ismay, never one to shy away from publicity, made

himself conspicuously available to the press. If he could not answer a question, he would quickly find someone who could. The White Star publicity machine was working overtime, sending out formal and informal invitations to the cream of society, entreating them to experience this new breed of luxury liner on its maiden voyage.

That the press was quick to pick up on the *Titanic* and, by association, her sister ships as being "unsinkable" proved to be a constant source of amusement for Ismay and the rest of the White Star Line. For, in point of fact, the word "unsinkable" had never appeared in any ads or promotional literature, the company preferring the more straightforward slogan "Largest and finest steamers in the world."

In the meantime, the *Olympic*, the first of the trio of luxury liners, was completed and set off on its first voyage in May 1911, at its helm veteran Captain Edward J. Smith. Captain Smith, known in the shipping industry as "the Millionaires' Captain" because of his popularity with wealthy owners, was an experienced seaman and a favorite of the White Star owners, who, in conversations among themselves, agreed that they would like to see him also pilot the *Titanic* on its first voyage.

Captain Smith's first voyage at the helm of one of the new ships of the White Star Line was an uneventful one. The *Olympic* performed admirably on its trip across the North Atlantic. There was a good run of calm seas to guide its passage and, as the ship steamed up the North (Hudson) River into New York, it pulled into the recently lengthened Pier No. 59.

As a group of 12 tugs began easing the *Olympic* into the dock, a sudden and totally unexpected reversal of the ship's starboard propeller sucked one of the tugs, the *O. L. Hallenback,* into the ship, causing extensive structural and rudder damage to the tug.

There were the inevitable charges and counter-charges. Tempers flared. Each side sued the other, and both suits were ultimately thrown out of court for lack of evidence. But suddenly there were whispers along the maritime grapevine.

Yes, luxury liners had grown to massive size. But had the experience necessary to handle these new monsters of the sea increased as well?

- The *Olympic's* hull is badly damaged in a collision with the Royal Navy cruiser *Hawke* on September 20, 1912. White Star workers are diverted to repair the *Olympic's* hull. The White Star Company announces a new date for the *Titanic's* first voyage: April 10, 1912.

- The *Titanic* is drydocked at Belfast's Thompson Graving Dock on February 3, 1912, in preparation for the coming sea trials.

- The first of the 321-member engineering crew board the *Titanic* in March 1912.

- Lifeboats are tested for the first time on March 25,

1912. The tests consist of raising and lowering the boats. The lifeboats pass all the tests.

- Captain Edward J. Smith turns 59 years old. He announces that the *Titanic*'s maiden voyage will be his last before retirement.

- The *Titanic*'s sea trials begin at 6 A.M. on April 2 in Belfast Lough. The ship passes various start-stop maneuvers and runs full speed at 20 knots. Later that day, the *Titanic* will run for two hours in open sea at an average speed of 18 knots. All the tests ultimately meet Board of Trade standards.

- Captain Bartlett, the first officer to captain the *Titanic*, leaves Belfast on April 12 at 8 P.M. for the 570-mile voyage from Belfast to Southampton, arriving just after midnight on April 3.

- The majority of the *Titanic* crew is recruited on April 6.

- The price of a first-class ticket is $3,100. The price of a third-class ticket is $32.

- A total of 559 tons of general cargo, including 11,524 separate pieces, 5,892 tons of coal, and one car, a Renault, are loaded on board.

- Food, drink, and related items are loaded on the *Titanic*. They include: 75,000 pounds of fresh meat, 35,000 fresh eggs, 40 tons of potatoes, 800 bundles of asparagus, 1,000 bottles of wine, 5,000 bottles of ale and stout, 12,000 dinner plates, 1,000 oyster forks, 15,000 champagne glasses, 40,000 towels and 45,000 table napkins.

• Captain Smith and his officers board the *Titanic* the evening of April 9 and spend their first night on board. The full crew boards the ship at 7:30 A.M. the following morning. A final lifeboat drill is held at 8 A.M.

• *Titanic*'s second- and third-class passengers arrive between 9:30 and 11 A.M. and board the ship. First-class passengers arrive and board at 11:30 A.M.

• Among the wealthy financiers and people of note sailing on the *Titanic* are John Jacob Astor, Benjamin Guggenheim, artist Frank Millet, editor W. T. Stead, writer Jacques Futrelle, theatrical producer Henry B. Harris, President William Howard Taft's military aide Colonel Archie Butt, and Isidor Straus, the owner of Macy's department store.

• J. P. Morgan, one of the world's richest men, books passage on the *Titanic* but changes his mind 24 hours before the ship departs.

• Passengers George Rosenshine and Maybelle Thorne travel as Mr. and Mrs. G. Thorne. They are not married but are traveling together and wish to avoid even a hint of impropriety.

• The passenger list also includes three professional card players traveling under assumed names. George

Bradley is listed as George Brayton, C. H. Romaine as C. Rolmane and Harry Homer as E. Haven.

• Lord Pirrie, one of the *Titanic*'s owners, is scheduled to be on the maiden voyage but comes down with pneumonia just days before she is to sail. He sends the ship's chief designer, Thomas Andrews, in his place.

• Edith Russell has originally booked passage on the ship *George Washington*, which is to leave on April 7. She switches to the *Titanic* when she learns its schedule will allow her a stopover in Paris.

When Edith Russell attempts to buy insurance on her luggage, she is told by Nicolas Martin, general manager of the White Star Line, that she need not worry about her luggage and that "this boat is unsinkable."

• A band plays the music "Britannia Rules the Waves" as the *Titanic* prepares to cast off.

• Moments before the *Titanic* is to cast off, seven members of the engine room crew race up to the ship and attempt to get on board. The officer on duty tells them they are too late and will not allow them on the ship.

• April 10, 1912, noon. The *Titanic* casts off from the Southampton docks and is towed out by six tugs into an area of deep waters known as River Test. During the casting-off procedure, water displaced by the *Titanic*'s movement causes the mooring ropes on the nearby American ship *New York* to break free. The *New York*'s stern swings out on a collision course with the *Titanic*. Quick maneuvering by Captain Smith avoids a collision by a mere four feet and causes a one-hour delay before the voyage finally gets underway.

• The first leg of the *Titanic* voyage, from Southampton to Cherbourg, France, covers 24 miles and takes four hours. During this leg of the trip a fire breaks out in boiler No. 5 but is quickly extinguished.

• Twenty-two passengers disembark at Cherbourg, and the ship takes on additional cargo. The *Titanic* takes on additional passengers and ups anchor at 8:10 P.M. for an uneventful trip through the English Channel and around England's southern coast.

• Driving to Cherbourg to catch a ride home on the *Titanic*, American Frank Carlson's car breaks down. He misses the boat.

• April 11, 1912, early morning. Captain Smith, still smarting from the near collision with the *New York* and with the memory of the *Olympic* mishap still fresh in his mind, puts the *Titanic* through additional maneuverability tests. All appears in order as the luxury liner prepares to drop anchor in Queenstown.

• The ship sits two miles out from Queenstown. A total of 113 third-class passengers and 7 second-class passengers embark. 1,385 bags of mail are also loaded on board. Seven passengers disembark. They are the Odell family, who had plans for a week of sightseeing along the Irish countryside. The *Titanic* weighs anchor for the last time and makes for the open sea on its way to New York.

• The *Titanic* is now carrying 1,316 passengers and 891 crew members.

• Captain Smith is informed that one crew member has deserted in Queenstown.

CHAPTER 4

PRELUDE TO DISASTER

The R.M.S. *Titanic* slipped easily through the waves on April 12, 1912. Captain Smith, feeling confident, passed word to the pilot and the engine room to execute some small maneuvers. They were nothing major, just some lazy S's as the *Titanic* laced deeper into open water. Fewer than 24 hours after spying the coast of Ireland for the last time, the passengers on the *Titanic* settled into a delightful routine.

The sun was out in full and there was nary a cloud in the sky. The water was calm. Passengers enjoyed strolls along the deck; there were mild flirtations between the single passengers; and days and nights could be spent listening and dancing to the White Star Line band. Games of chance were very much in evidence and, although mild warnings had been posted to warn passengers that professional gamblers were probably on board, they did little to deter eager players.

First-class passengers were quick to look up acquaintances, as this was a crowd that regularly traveled in the same circles. They got together in the luxurious restaurants and reception areas for meals and drinks, and to swap the latest bit of gossip or business news. One thing they all agreed on was that J. P. Morgan had put his money where his mouth was: The *Titanic* was truly a marvel of the age.

Colonel Archibald Gracie soon emerged as one of the more congenial members of first-class society and could regularly be counted on to compliment the ladies and make interesting small talk with the men over a good cigar and a glass of ale. Helen Churchill Candee, a writer of some note in polite society, would often offer up a sharp wit and obvious intelligence that drew a number of single men to her table at every meal and after-dinner concert. She had struck up varying degrees of friendship during the early days of the voyage but had found particular favorites in Hugh Woolner, the son of a noted English sculptor, and architect Edward A. Kent.

The motion picture industry, barely a blip on society's consciousness in 1912, was fairly well represented on *Titanic*'s first voyage. Dorothy Gibson, returning from holiday in Europe with her mother, had emerged as one of the silent era's first legitimate stars. Daniel M. Marvin, cutting quite the figure in the smoking room and lounges, was the son of Henry N. Marvin, president of the Biograph Company.

But the truest indication that *Titanic* had arrived as a full-blown Hollywood event was the ever-present camera of Noel Malachard. Malachard, on assignment from Pathé Weekly, the newsreel company, was everywhere, capturing the smiles, the events, and the endless good times aboard the *Titanic* as it cleaved through the waters on the way to New York.

Inside his cabin, designer Thomas Andrews continued to be all business in regard to his creation. Laboring over blueprints and handwritten notes, Andrews was already looking to the future of the *Titanic* and ships like her.

One set of detailed designs called for the reduction of the number of screws in stateroom hat racks. Another exceedingly detailed outline called for staining all the wicker furniture in the Café Parisien green. Somewhere in this jumble was the latest missive from Andrews's wife, Helen, with the latest news about their child.

One more note, buried near the bottom of the dense and seemingly disorganized pile, would have to be addressed when the *Titanic* got to New York. It was a message from Second Officer Lightoller, requesting binoculars for the lookouts on the return trip to England.

By 1:30 P.M. on April 12, the *Titanic* had covered 386 nautical miles. The crew was operating at a polished professional level, and there were no problems. Captain Smith was pleased. He was well aware that a record existed on the transatlantic course they were on and, while not stating publicly that he was pushing the *Titanic* to break that record on its maiden voyage, the good weather and the ability to keep at a better than 20-knot speed did make breaking that record a possibility. The only break in the revelry and easy times would come in a matter of hours and would go unnoticed by all except Captain Smith and Fourth Officer Boxhall.

It was a message from the French liner *La Touraine* warning that there was ice ahead.

• The *La Touraine* message indicates the ice is a thousand miles away and to the north. Captain Smith sees no danger and does not heed the warning.

• On the night of April 13, the *Titanic* receives a light blinker warning from a passing ship, the *Rappahannock*, which reports damage from an encounter with a heavy ice floe (a twisted rudder and a dented bow). The *Titanic* flashes back a response and continues on.

• A Church of England Sunday service is held after breakfast on April 14.

• April 14. 9 A.M. Fourth Officer Boxhall receives a message from the ship *Caronia* which reads "Bergs, growlers, and field ice in latitude 42° N. from longitude 49° to 51' W." Boxhall writes the word "ice" on a slip of paper with the *Caronia*'s message underneath and tucks the slip of paper into a frame of the chart room table. Captain Smith is given the message and the coordinates are marked off on the chart.

- 1:42 P.M. Captain Smith receives a message from the liner *Baltic*, reporting ice at latitude 40° 51' N., longitude 49° 52' W. Captain Smith writes down the information, puts it in his pocket and goes about his business. Later that day he runs into White Star Line Managing Director Bruce Ismay and gives the note to him. Ismay will regale a number of passengers with the note and the idea that there are icebergs ahead before stuffing the note in his pocket. Ismay will later give the note back to Captain Smith, but the message is never posted.

- Yet another "ice ahead" warning is received in the late afternoon from the ship *Noordam*. The particulars of that message are not known. Captain Smith reportedly takes the message and does not post it.

- 1:45 P.M. Another ice warning, hot on the heels of the *Baltic*, from the *Amerika,* reporting ice at latitude 41° 27' N., longitude 50° 8' W. To this point, the *Titanic* officers believed that the ice is off to the north. But the *Amerika* message and those that will follow place the ice to the south and directly in their path.

- The warm, sunny temperature suddenly turns cold. By 7:30 P.M. the temperature has fallen to 39° F.

- 7:30 P.M. A message is received by Second Wireless Operator Harold Bride from the ship *Californian*. Citing the coordinates latitude 42° 3' N., longitude 49° 9' W., the message reads "Three large bergs five miles to the southward of us." Bride takes the message to the bridge but will later recall that he does not remember who he gave it to. The ice is now only 50 miles ahead.

• The dinner menu on the night of April 14 includes: Filet Mignon, Sauté of Chicken, Lamb in Mint Sauce, Roast Duckling, Sirloin of Beef, Green Peas, Creamed Carrots, Boiled Rice, Roast Squab, Cold Asparagas Vinaigrette, Waldorf Pudding, Chocolate and Vanilla Eclairs, and French Ice Cream.

• 9 P.M. The temperature has dropped to 33°F.

• Captain Smith retires for the evening at 9:25 P.M. His parting orders to Second Officer Lightoller are: "If it becomes at all doubtful, let me know at once."

• 9:30 P.M. Second Officer Lightoller warns the lookouts to watch out for ice.

• 9:40 P.M. The *Titanic* receives a message from the Atlantic transport *Mesaba*. The message reads, "latitude 42° N. to 41° 25' N., longitude 40° W. to 50° 30' W. Saw much heavy pack ice and a great number of large icebergs, also field ice." Legend has it that First Wireless Operator John Phillips takes this message and promptly puts it under a paperweight, where it is never seen. Later inquiries indicate that Phillips did pass it on to the bridge sometime after Second Officer Lightoller went off duty . . . and that the message was ignored. At this point, the *Titanic* is well inside the "danger zone" of the ice field and, unbeknownst to its crew, will continue to travel through it for two hours without even a scrape.

- 10:30 P.M. The temperature has dipped to 31°.

- In the lookout nest, Reginald Lee and Frederick Fleet complain that they have not been supplied with binoculars. Fleet's eyes have not been tested in five years. Lee's eyes have not been tested in 13 years.

- 11 P.M. First Wireless Operator John Phillips, attempting to get a backlog of outgoing messages out through his hookup with Cape Race, Newfoundland, is interrupted by another, more frantic message from the *Californian* which, at this time, is between 10 and 19 miles north of the *Titanic*. The message is: "I say, old man, we're stopped and surrounded by ice." Before the *Californian* can give its coordinates, an irritated Phillips shouts back, "Shut up! Shut up! I'm busy! I'm working Cape Race!" and cuts off the *Californian*'s message. The *Californian*'s wireless operator would stay on the line and monitor the *Titanic*'s wireless line for another 30 minutes in an attempt to get through and complete his warning. Finally, at 11:30 P.M., the *Californian*'s wireless operator shuts off his set and goes to bed.

- 11:30 P.M. The *Titanic* is proceeding along at cruising speed of $22^1/2$ knots, moving at a rate of 38 feet per second.

- 11:40 P.M. Lookout Fleet spots an iceberg approximately 500 yards ahead. Its height is approximately 60 feet. He clangs the crow's nest bell three times and immediately gets on the phone with a three-word message: "Iceberg right ahead!"

CHAPTER 5

THE SINKING
OF THE *TITANIC*

*I*n a matter of seconds, the bridge and the engine
room were scenes of confusion. It is still some-
what unclear, years later, which orders to
avoid catastrophe were given, and in what sequence.

Lookout Fleet had been warned earlier in the evening to be on the lookout for icebergs. But it appeared
to have been a false alarm. Nothing had loomed out of
the darkness. Ironically, the clear, calm air and water
made icebergs especially difficult to detect, since there
were no breakers to reveal the base of the bergs.

What is known is that the warning went from the
crow's nest to the bridge and finally to the engine room.
The *Titanic*'s chain of command regarding such unexpected situations was absolutely by the book.

Seconds after he heard Fleet's report, First Officer
Murdoch sent a message to the engine room and
ordered the engines to be reversed: "Full speed astern!"
Then, as Quartermaster Hitchens later testified at the
U.S. Senate hearings following the disaster, Murdoch
ordered him to turn the wheel "hard a' starboard" to

avoid the iceberg. That meant turning the stern of the ship to starboard and the bow to port. At the same hearings, Quartermaster Olliver remembered that seconds later he heard Murdoch order "Hard aport!", which would have reversed the direction of the helm.

Marine experts have since claimed that if the ship had simply hit the ship head on, she would have been injured but not mortally wounded. Only two or three of her watertight compartments would have filled with water, and the strong stem of the ship would have absorbed most of the impact. Instead, by following his instincts and trying to avoid the berg when the ship was practically on top of it, Murdoch assured that the ice would do the utmost damage.

Olliver also swore that Captain Smith came running out of his quarters after the *Titanic* hit the berg and ordered the ship to proceed "half speed ahead." It is not sure how long the ship might have kept going, if indeed she did.

In the crow's nest before the collision, Fleet and Lee could do nothing but watch as the massive chunk of ice bore down on them. The pair of lookouts said silent prayers.

As the bow of the *Titanic* suddenly began to twist to the port side, Fleet was sure that it would be a very close call.

In the lounge, Dorothy Gibson and her mother were playing bridge with fellow passengers William T. Sloper and Fred Seward. A steward came by and told them he would have to turn out the lights in the lounge. The group begged him to let them finish the rubber. Shortly after the cards were thrown on the table, they head a loud, sickening, crashing sound.

11:40 P.M. to 12:45 A.M.

- 11:40 P.M. Sixth Officer Moody receives Fleet's warning and relays it to First Officer Murdoch. He yells "hard a-starboard" to the helmsman, who turns the wheel while Murdoch activates the lever that will close the watertight doors.

- Thirty-seven seconds after Fleet's frantic call to the bridge, the *Titanic* strikes the iceberg, producing a series of irregular gashes, from bow to starboard, for a length of 300 feet. The impact punctures several of the 16 watertight compartments, which, when filled with air, were designed to keep the *Titanic* afloat.

- Passengers, upon hearing the news, are curious and playful rather than fearful and immediately repair to the starboard side of the *Titanic*, where chunks of the iceberg have fallen on deck, and begin throwing chunks of ice at each other.

- 11:50 P.M. The first signs of trouble. Water has risen 14 feet above the keel. Five watertight compartments begin to take on water. Boiler room No. 6 is flooded with eight feet of water. Approximately 4,000 cubic feet of water flood into the *Titanic* during the first ten minutes after being hit by the iceberg. Approximately 24,000 cubic feet of water entered the *Titanic* during the first hour after the collision.

• 11:55 P.M. Second Wireless Operator Bride relieves First Wireless Operator Phillips. Phillips informs Bride that the ship "has somehow been damaged" and that they'll have to return to Belfast.

• Third-class passengers Carl Johnson and David Buckley are two of the first passengers to notice any trouble. Both get out of their bunks and discover water seeping into their staterooms up to their ankles.

• 12 midnight. Captain Smith and Harland and Wolff director Thomas Andrews meet on the bridge and do a quick tour of the damaged areas. They discover that water is pouring into the mailroom and into No. 1, 2 and 3 holds. After the tour, Andrews tells Smith he gives the *Titanic* "from an hour to an hour and a half" before it sinks. Phillips reports to Captain Smith and asks whether he should begin sending the regulation distress code "CQD." Captain Smith replies, "Yes, at once!"

• An argument breaks out on C Deck between a passenger and a steward. The passenger has broken open a compartment door to free a friend who was trapped when the crash occurred. The steward is yelling that the passenger will have to pay for damages.

- Phillips and Andrews notice that the stairs to A Deck are out of balance and that the *Titanic* seems to be listing to port.

- Andrews and Phillips run into stewardess Mary Sloan on the way back to the bridge. Andrews gives Sloan the following message: "It's very serious. But keep the news quiet. I don't want a panic."

- 12:00 A.M. The *Titanic's* chief purser empties out the first- and second-class safes of valuables and begins handing them back to the passengers.

- April 15. 12:05 A.M. Phillips sends the first distress message with the *Titanic's* estimated position being latitude 41° 46' N., longitude 50° 14' W. The *Titanic's* squash court, 32 feet above the water line, is now flooding. Captain Smith gives the order to uncover the lifeboats and to muster the crew and passengers. Smith, to his horror, realizes that, even if every boat is filled, there will only be enough room for 1,178 of the 2,227 people on board. Each lifeboat, fully loaded, weighs five and a half tons.

- 12:10 A.M. Third Officer Charles V. Groves, aboard the *Californian*, makes several attempts to contact the "mystery ship" whose lights have been spotted. He makes several unsuccessful attempts to contact the ship by way of Morse lamp but fails. He attempts to make the wireless receiver work but is unfamiliar with the equipment and fails. Finally he gives up and goes to bed. Consequently the *Californian*, only a handful of miles away, misses the *Titanic*'s first message.

- 12:10 A.M. Fourth Officer Boxhall awakens Second Officer Lightoller with the news, "You know we have struck an iceberg." To which Lightoller responds, "I know we have struck something." Lightoller dresses as Boxhall informs him that the water is already up to F Deck.

- 12:15 to 12:17 A.M. The *Titanic*'s distress call is picked up by her sister ship *Olympic*, which, at the time, is 500 miles away. A number of other ships including *Mount Temple* (49 miles away), *Frankfort* (153 miles), *Birma* (70 miles), *Baltic* (243 miles), *Virginian* (170 miles), and *Carpathia* (58 miles) pick up the distress call and prepare to come to the *Titanic*'s aid.

- At 12:15 A.M. the band, under orders to do what they can to calm any panic, begins playing a set of ragtime tunes in the first-class lounge on A Deck.

- 12:18 A.M. The first ship to reply is the *Frankfort*. Their message to the *Titanic* is "OK . . . stand by."

- 12:20 A.M. Water begins to flood through the seamen's quarters. E Deck is flooding. Water level has now risen to 48 feet above the keel.

- 12:25 A.M. First Wireless Operator Phillips receives a message from the *Carpathia*. The operator, seemingly unaware of the *Titanic*'s predicament, exchanges a few pleasantries before the exasperated *Titanic* operator shouts "Come at once! We've struck a berg!" There were tense moments of silence as the operator sends for his captain. By 12:30 A.M., the *Carpathia* operator is back on the line with the news that "the *Carpathia* is only 58 miles away and running hard."

- 12:40 A.M. A rumor begins circulating that men are being taken off on the port side of the ship. Many believe it. It is later reported that the rumor was started by the three cardsharps in order to make their escape on the starboard side easier.

- 12:45 A.M. In a desperate move, Wireless Operator Phillips begins sending out the newly created international call for distress. At that moment the distress call S.O.S. is sent out for the first time in history.

12:45 A.M. to 1:30 A.M.

- 12:45 A.M. The first distress rocket is fired from the deck of the *Titanic*. Ten miles away it is spotted by the *Californian*'s Second Officer Herbert Stone. The *Californian*, amazingly, has still not received any of the *Titanic*'s distress calls.

- 12:45 A.M. First-class passenger J. R. McGough is walking by lifeboat No. 7 when First Officer Murdoch grabs him by the shoulders and gives him a push. He tells McGough "Here, you're a big fellow. You can row. Get in the boat."

- Across the way from lifeboat No. 7, gym instructor T. W. McCawley is showing passengers how to use the gymnasium equipment. The passengers seem more interested in that than in what is going on at lifeboat No. 7.

- 12:45 A.M. The *Titanic*'s passengers are still not taking the collision seriously, and so when Captain Smith calls for the first lifeboat, No. 7, to be filled and lowered into the cold Atlantic, and First Officer Murdoch makes the first call, only a handful of passengers get in the boat. Lifeboat No. 7 has a capacity of 65. It leaves the *Titanic* with only 28 passengers on board.

- Shortly after lifeboat No. 7 is in the water, it is discovered that a plug at the bottom of the boat is not fitting properly and that it is in danger of springing a leak, and that there are no food, water, lanterns, or matches on board. Passengers would take turns sitting on the plug to keep it in place.

- 12:45 A.M. Captain Smith orders lifeboat No. 4 to be loaded. Passengers are all ready to board when Captain Smith realizes that he has forgotten that the Boat Deck, where the lifeboat lies, is surrounded by glass windows that have not been opened. The passengers are herded down to the Promenade Deck while orders are given to get the windows open.

- John Jacob Astor sits quietly with his wife, securing a lifejacket around her, telling her everything is going to be all right.

- 12:55 A.M. First Officer Murdoch has moved to lifeboat No. 5 and is calling for passengers. One group hovering nearby consists of Mr. and Mrs. Richard Beckwith, Mr. and Mrs. E. N. Kimball, Miss Helen Newsom, and Karl H. Behr. They are hesitant to get into the boat. Bruce Ismay comes upon the group and urges them to get on board. Finally Mrs. Beckwith approaches Ismay and asks if their whole group can go together. Ismay, not thinking of the "women and children first" edict that has been passed along from Captain Smith, says, "Of course, madam, every one of you." Boat No. 5 is lowered with 41 passengers aboard out of a capacity for 65. Fifth Officer Lowe, who is present at lifeboat No. 5, argues with Ismay and warns him to stop interfering with the command of the ship.

- 12:55 A.M. Concern is beginning to spread among the passengers and crew. Fearing the worst, Chief Officer Wilde, First Officer Murdoch, and Second Officer Lightoller race to the firearms chest and break out handguns. Wilde, at one point, pushes a handgun into Lightoller's hand and reportedly says, "You may need it."

- 12:55 A.M. Amid the confusion, lifeboat No. 6 is lowered with only 28 passengers aboard. Among them is one Molly Brown, who will, in later years, become known as "The Unsinkable Molly Brown."

- 1:00 A.M. Lifeboat No. 3 (capacity 65) is launched with only 32 aboard. Of that total, 11 are crew members.

- 1:05 A.M. Phillips and Bride notice the floor of the *Titanic* beginning to tilt. Phillips, in a classic bit of understatement, suggests to Bride, "I think we're in a tight pickle." Bride's response? "You think we'll be having sand for breakfast?"

- 1:10 A.M. In easily the worst case of a boat leaving the *Titanic* with too few people, First Officer Murdoch, after repeated calls for women and children first, allows lifeboat No. 1, capacity 40, to leave with a total of 12, five passengers and seven crewmen. Of that total, two are women, and there are no children.

- Crew member Walter Hurst, watching as No. 1 swung down past him on the way to the ocean, remarks, "If they are sending the boats away, they might as well put some people in them."

- 12:30 A.M. to 1:15 A.M. Third Class Steward John Edward Hart makes numerous trips down into the third-class section of the ship, leads a number of passengers up to the lifeboats, and assists them with their lifejackets.

- At the same moment that lifeboat No. 1 is being lowered, lifeboat No. 8, with a total of 39 people aboard, is being lowered under the supervision of Captain Smith and Second Officer Lightoller. There are still approximately 30 seats left, and the women are screaming that some of their husbands be allowed on. But Captain Smith, sticking to his "women and children first" edict, refuses. Given the lack of an experienced helmsman on the boat, the Countess of Rothes, with no nautical experience, bravely takes the tiller and moves the boat away from the *Titanic*. An unidentified steward in No. 8 reportedly tells a fellow passenger, "I've never had an oar in my hand before but I think I can row."

- 1:15 A.M. The *Titanic* continues to fire its distress rockets. But they explode too close to the deck and there is not enough light to indicate a distress signal. The *Californian* continues to ignore them.

- 1:15 A.M. The water has reached the *Titanic*'s name on the bow.

- Thomas Andrews warns the engine crew that, in a little more than an hour, "the wall will become the floor and all the machinery will break loose."

- 1:20 A.M. Third Class Steward John Edward Hart has made one final trip down to third class and has emerged with a number of passengers in tow at lifeboat No. 15, where First Class Officer Murdoch, after loading 69 passengers and crew on board, orders Hart into the boat.

- Lifeboat No. 9 leaves at 1:20 A.M. with 56 people on board.

- 1:25 A.M. Lifeboat No. 12, containing 40 women and children and two seamen, is lowered into the water.

- 1:25 A.M. First Wireless Operator John Phillips receives the following message from the *Olympic*: "Are you steering south to meet us?" Phillips, outraged at the fact that the *Olympic* does not seem to understand the gravity of the situation, patiently explains, "We are putting the women off in the boats."

- 1:30 A.M. Panic erupts at lifeboat No. 14. Fifth Officer Lowe draws his gun on a young boy and orders him out. He gets out of the boat. Moments later lifeboat No. 14 is swinging out over the water. A group of men rush the lifeboat, attempting to jump in. Seaman Scarrott beats them off with the tiller. Fifth Officer Lowe once again pulls his gun and shouts, "If anyone else tries that, this is what he'll get!" Lowe fires three shots along the side of the ship. The crowd backs off as lifeboat No. 14 with its 60 passengers, including Fifth Officer Lowe, is lowered into the water.

- 1:30 A.M. First Wireless Officer John Phillips continues to send out frantic distress calls to any ships in the area. One of his last is, "We are sinking fast. Women and children in boats. Cannot last much longer."

1:30 A.M. to 2:00 A.M.

- 1:30 A.M. Lifeboats Nos. 13, 15, and 16 are being loaded. Nos. 13 and 16 are loaded with a minimum amount of confusion. But a problem arises at 15 when a group of men rush the boat. Officer Murdoch beats back the crowd, yelling, "Stand back! Stand back! It's women first!"

- 1:30 A.M. The panic continues as the *Titanic* crew tries to get lifeboat Collapsible C uncovered and ready to load. A mob rushes the boat, attempting to climb into it. Purser Herbert McElroy pulls a gun and fires two shots into the air. "Get out of this! Clear out of this!" Two men manage to climb into the boat. Two passengers, Hugh Woolner and Bjornstrom Steffanson, see the gunshot flashes, hear McElroy's screams and rush to his aid. They yank the two men out of the boat. The loading continues.

- 1:35 A.M. Lifeboat No. 16 is lowered with approximately 50 people on board. No. 13 leaves moments later with 64 people, mostly women and children, on board. No. 15, with 70 passengers aboard, is lowered immediately after 13 and is lowered right on top of 13. A tragic collision is narrowly averted when lifeboat 13 pulls out of the way just in the nick of time.

- 1:40 A.M. Chief Officer Wilde, in a frantic attempt to at least temporarily right the deck, shouts out, "Everyone on the starboard side to straighten her up!" The passengers and crew move, and the *Titanic* swings back to even keel.

- 1:40 A.M. Lifeboat Collapsible C is filling up. Chief

Officer Wilde shouts out the question, "Who is in command of this boat?" Captain Smith, who is also supervising the loading of Collapsible C, turns to Quartermaster Rowe, who had been helping with the loading and declares him in charge. Rowe jumps into the boat and the lowering begins.

• Just as Collapsible C is going over the side, White Star ship director J. Bruce Ismay jumps in. Another rush of passengers approaches Collapsible C but are stopped dead in their tracks when First Officer Murdoch fires two shots in the air. Two passengers attempt to leap into the boat from the deck above but are thrown out. Collapsible C leaves the *Titanic* with 42 people on board.

• Witnesses will later testify that First Officer Murdoch did not fire in the air but actually shot at and killed two passengers. Then he reportedly turned the gun on himself and committed suicide.

• 1:45 A.M. The forward Well Deck of the *Titanic* is now under water. Lifeboat No. 2, with a capacity of 40, leaves with only 25 passengers on board.

• 1:45 A.M. The *Carpathia* is steaming toward the *Titanic* at top speed. First Wireless Operator Russell continues on the bridge, sending distress calls. The last message the *Carpathia* gets from the *Titanic* reads, "Engine room full up to boilers."

- 1:45 A.M. John Jacob Astor asks Officer Lightoller if he can join his wife in Lifeboat No. 4. Lightoller reply, "No, sir. No men are allowed in these boats until the women are loaded in first."

- Another conflict arises on No. 4. When Mrs. Arthur Ryerson attempts to get her son, Jack, on the boat, Lightoller blocks the way, shouting, "That boy can't go!" Arthur Ryerson steps forward and confronts Lightoller, screaming, "Of course that boy goes with his mother. He is only thirteen." Lightoller relents and lets them pass, but not before he grumbles, "No more boys."

- 1:55 A.M. Lifeboat No. 4 is lowered with 40 women and children on board. In the rush to get the boat off, it leaves with 20 empty seats.

- 2:00 A.M. The crew attempts to get Collapsible boats A and B off the roof of the officers' quarters. But their inaccessibility and location make them difficult to move.

- 2:00 A.M. The water level has now risen to the Promenade Deck.

- 2:00 A.M. There are still more than 1,500 passengers and crew left on the *Titanic*.

- 2:00 A.M. One lifeboat remains, the Collapsible D. It has only 47 seats.

2:00 A.M. to 2:20 A.M.

- 2:00 A.M. Officer Lightoller heads up the loading of Collapsible D. To head off the inevitable rush on the boat, he has the crew members form a circle around the boat and lock arms. Only women and children are allowed through the circle. The expected rush on the last boat is stopped when Lightoller pulls his gun and fires two shots into the air.

- Mrs. Isidor Straus refuses to enter a lifeboat without her husband, stating "We have been living together for many years. Where you go I go."

- Benjamin Guggenheim, standing near a lifeboat as it is prepared to be lowered, asks a passenger to tell his wife that he went down like a gentleman.

- 2:00 A.M. A man calling himself Mr. Hoffman approaches Collapsible D and hands over two baby boys before disappearing back into the crowd. It will later be determined that his real name is Navatril and that he had kidnapped his two children from his estranged wife.

- 2:05 A.M. Frederick Hoyt makes sure his wife is safely in the boat. As the Collapsible D is lowered over the side, with 44 passengers on board, Hoyt jumps overboard and swims to a spot he thinks the lifeboat will pass.

- 2:05 A.M. The forecastle of the *Titanic* sinks below the water.

- 2:10 A.M. The Collapsible D rows past the spot where Frederick Hoyt is swimming and he is hauled aboard.

- 2:10 A.M. Captain Smith enters the bridge where Wireless Operators Phillips and Bride are still sending distress signals. He reportedly tells them, "Men, you have done your full duty. You can do no more. Abandon your cabin. Now it's every man for himself." Phillips will continue sending out the last distress calls for another seven minutes.

- 2:17 A.M. Captain Smith does a quick tour of the decks, officially releasing his crew with the order, "Every man for himself." He returns to the bridge, determined, in the grand tradition of the sea, to go down with his ship.

- *Titanic* shipbuilder Thomas Andrews retires to the first-class smoking lounge, where he stares silently off into space.

- 2:17 A.M. Father Thomas Byles hears confession and gives absolution to more than 100 passengers.

- 2:17 A.M. As Wireless Operators Phillips and Bride are preparing to leave the bridge for the last time, a crew member enters and attempts to steal Phillips's life-jacket. A fight breaks out. Phillips knocks the crewman unconscious.

- 2:17 A.M. The band stops playing and joins the remaining passengers and crew as they jump overboard.

- 2:17 A.M. Collapsible boats A and B slide off the roof and into the water upside down as the *Titanic* is now standing nearly perpendicular in the water. Dozens of crewmen and passengers swim to them and grab hold.

- 2:18 A.M. A loud roar echoes through the night. The ship breaks in two. The bow half sinks.

- 2:20 A.M. After one or two minutes, the stern begins to slip under. The remains of the *Titanic* vanish into the sea.

- 2:20 A.M. Fireman Harry Senior reported that shortly after the *Titanic* sank, he saw the body of Captain Smith, holding a baby in his arms, floating motionless in the ocean.

- A total of 60 percent, or 199, of the first-class passengers were saved. A total of 25 percent, or 174, of the third-class passengers survived. Only 32 percent of the total passengers and crew on the *Titanic* were saved.

LIFEBOAT PASSENGER LIST

It took months to sort out who exactly got off the *Titanic* and in which lifeboat they made their escape. In one of the first books of any substance about the *Titanic*, *The Truth About the Titanic,* by Colonel Archibald Gracie, the passengers were put in their places for the first time. You'll note that most of the passengers Colonel Gracie was able to identify were either first-class passengers, like himself, or crew members.

PORT SIDE LIFEBOATS
BOAT NO. 6
Miss Bowerman, Mrs. J. J. Brown, Mrs. Candee, Mrs. Cavendish, Miss Barber, Mrs. Meyer, Miss Norton, Mrs. Rothschild, Mrs. L. P. Smith, Mrs. Stone, Miss Icard, Q. M. Hitchins, Seaman Fleet, an unidentified boy with an injured arm.

BOAT NO. 8
Mrs. Bucknell, Albina Bazzani, Miss Cherry, Mrs. Kenyon, Miss Leader, Mrs. Pears, Mrs. Penasco, Mlle. Olivia, Countess Rothes, Miss Maloney, Mrs. Swift, Mrs. Taussig, Miss Taussig, Mrs. White, Amelia Bessetti, Mrs. Wick, Miss Wick, Miss Young, Ellen Bird, Seaman T. Jones, Stewards Crawford and Hart, an unidentified cook.

BOAT NO. 10
Miss Andrews, Miss Longley, Mrs. Hogeboom, Mrs. Parrish, Mrs. Shelley, Seamen Buley and Evans, Fireman Rice, Steward Burke, 41 unidentified women, 7 unidentified children, 2 unidentified male passengers, and 1 unidentified crewman.

BOAT NO. 12
Miss Phillips, Seaman Poigndestre, F. Clench, 40 unidentified women and children passengers, and 1 unidentified male passenger.

BOAT NO. 14
Mrs. Compton, Miss Compton, Mrs. Minahan, Miss

Minahan, Mrs. Collyer, Miss Collyer, C. Williams, Fifth Officer Lowe, Seaman Scarrot, Stewards Crowe, Stewart, and Morris, 42 unidentified women passengers, 1 unidentified male passenger, 2 unidentified crew members.

BOAT NO. 16
Master at Arms Bailey, Seaman Archer, Steward Andrews, Stewardess Leather, 2 unidentified crew members, and 50 unidentified women and children passengers.

BOAT NO. 2
Miss Allen, Mrs. Appleton, Mrs. Cornell, Mrs. Douglas, Miss Le Roy, Miss Madill, Mrs. Robert, Amelia Kenchen, Brahim Youssef, Hanne Youssef, Marian Youssef, Georges Youssef, Fourth Officer Boxhall, Seaman Osman, Steward Johnston, 9 unidentified passengers, and 1 unidentified cook.

BOAT NO. 4
Mrs. Astor, Miss Bidois, Miss Bowen, Mrs. Carter, Miss Serepeca, Mrs. Clark, Mrs. Cummings, Miss Eustis, Mrs. Ryerson and her two children, Miss S.R., Miss E., Master J.B., Chandowson, Mrs. Stephenson, Mrs. Thayer and maid, Mrs. Widener and maid, Q. M. Perkis, Seamen McCarthy, Hemmings, and Lyons, Storekeepers Foley and Prentice, Firemen Smith and Dillion, Greasers Granger and Scott, Stewards Cunningham and Siebert, 1 unidentified male passenger, 16 unidentifed women and children passengers.

COLLAPSIBLE BOAT D

Mrs. J. M. Brown, Mrs. Harris, Mrs. Frederick Hoyt, Michel and Edmund Navratil, Frederik Hoyt, Joseph Dugemin, H. B. Steffanson, H. Woolner, Q. M. Bright, Seaman Lucas, Steward Hardy, 35 unidentified women and children passengers.

COLLAPSIBLE BOAT B

A. H. Barkworth, Archibald Gracie, John B. Thayer Jr., Second Officer Lightoller, Wireless Operator Bride, Firemen McGann and Senior, Chief Baker Joughin, Cooks Collins and Maynard, Steward Whiteley, J. Hagan, Seaman J. McGough.

STARBOARD SIDE LIFEBOATS
BOAT NO. 7

Mmes. Bishop, Earnshaw, Gibson, Greenfield, Potter, and Snyder, Miss Gibson, Miss Hayes, Mrs. Dodge and child, Messrs. Bishop, Chevre, Daniel, Greenfield, McGough, Marechal, Seward, Sloper, Snyder, Tucker, Calderhead and Flynn, Seamen Hogg, Jewell, and Weller.

BOAT NO. 5

Mmes. Cassebeer, Chambers, Crosby, Dodge and her child, Frauenthal, Goldenberg, Harder, Kimball, Stehli, Stengel, Taylor and Warren, Misses Crosby, Newson, Ostby, and Frolicher Stehli, Messrs. Beckwith, Behr, Calderhead, Chambers, Flynn, Goldenberg, Harder, Kimball, Stehli, Taylor, Dr. Frauenthal, Isaac P. Mauge, Third Officer Pitman, Seaman Oliver, Fireman Shiers,

Stewards Edwards, Etches, and Guy, an unidentified stewardess, and 4 unidentified passengers.

BOAT NO. 3
Mmes. Cardeza and maid, Anna Hard, Davidson, Dick, Graham, Harper, Hayes and maid, Misses Pericault, Spedden and maid, Helen Wilson and son Douglas and nurse Miss Burns, Miss Graham, Miss Shutes, Messrs. Cardeza and manservant Lesneur, Dick, Harper and manservants Hamad Hassah and Spedden, Seaman Moore, Forward Pascoe, Steward McKay, 5 unidentified passengers, and 12 unidentified crewmen.

BOAT NO. 1
Lady Duff Gordon and maid, Miss Francatelli, Lord Duff Gordon, Messrs. Solomon and Stengel, Seamen Symons and Horswell, Firemen Collins, Hendrickson, Pusey, Shee, and Taylor.

BOAT NO. 9
Mmes. Aubert and maid, Mlle. Segesser, Futrelle, Lines, Miss Lines, Seamen Haines, Wynne, Q. M. McGough, and Peters, Stewards Ward, and Widgery, and 45 unidentified passengers and crewmen.

BOAT NO. 11
Mrs. Schabert, Mr. Mock, Seamen Humphreys and Brice, Stewards Wheate, MacKay, McMicken, Thessinger, and Wheelton, Stewardess Mrs. Robinson, 59 unidentified passengers, and 1 unidentified crewman.

BOAT NO. 13

Mrs. Caldwell and her child Alden, Dr. Dodge, Messrs. Beasley and Caldwell, Firemen Barrett, Beauchamp, Major, Stewards Ray and Wright, and 54 unidentified passengers and crewmen.

BOAT NO. 15

Mr. Haven, Fireman Diamond, Cavell, Taylor, Stewards Rule and Hart, 53 unidentified passengers and 11 unidentified crewmen.

COLLAPSIBLE BOAT C

J. Bruce Ismay, Mr. Carter, Quartermaster Rowe, Steward Pearce, Barber Weikman, 31 unidentified passengers, and 3 unidentified crewmen.

COLLAPSIBLE BOAT A

T. Beattie, P. D. Daly, G. Rheims, R. N. Williams Jr., O. Abelseth, W. J. Mellers, Mrs. Rosa Abbott, Edward Lindley, Steward E. Brown, Fireman J. Thompson, and 3 unidentified passengers.

CHAPTER 6

IN THE WATER

There were screams as the mighty ship went down:

"Row like hell or we'll get the devil of a swell."

"Pull for your lives or you'll be sucked under."

Inside the lifeboats, hands, many unaccustomed to manual labor, grabbed for the oars and pulled for dear life. When there were not enough men in a boat, women were quick to pick up the oars. Class and wealth had no meaning at a time like this. Survival in the waters of the North Atlantic was suddenly the great equalizer.

A gray vapor hung over the night sky as the last of the *Titanic* sank beneath the waves. The sea was littered with a mixture of unrecognizable garbage and more familiar objects such as deck chairs, remnants of the good life on a dream voyage that had suddenly turned, vividly, into a nightmare.

And for the hundreds of passengers who had jumped in time or managed to avoid being sucked down with the ship by grabbing onto a ship's railing or an oar—

55

or, as in one case, by lashing one's body to a wooden door—the horror was only beginning. The water temperature at the moment the *Titanic* went down was 28 degrees, well below freezing and, as many would discover, it was a ticking time bomb that would overcome the less hardy in a matter of minutes.

And then there were the screams in the night, screams of pain, terror, and prayer to God for deliverance from this freezing hell. Bodies would occasionally bob to the surface and roll silently in the waves. Those still alive swam frantically in all directions, driven by fear and by the hope that this way meant a lifeboat, a helping hand, and warm salvation. A few got lucky. The overwhelming majority swam until they died.

In the lifeboats there were lamentations as well, cries of loss for a husband or child and of fear at an uncertain future.

Some of those still alive adopted a stiff upper lip, shouting encouragement and offering up orders to "row hard" as a possible means to survival. Some had their doubts and were already making their peace with the Almighty. Others trusted that help was on the way.

The first rescue ship on the scene, the *Carpathia*, would not arrive until 4:10 A.M. For the next two hours the survivors of the *Titanic* would fight for life. It was a fight, based on reports handed down over the years, that would be played out in big and small moments of heroism, cowardice, and horror, and in biting bits of ironic humor. When exactly the following events happened is not important.

Because, for the survivors of the *Titanic*, time had suddenly stood still.

- While in the water, a third-class passenger, one Olaus Abelseth, is attacked by a panic-stricken man who grabs him around the neck. Fearing he will be dragged down, Abelseth kicks the man and drives him away. Twenty minutes later, Abselseth spots lifeboat Collapsible A bobbing in the water and hauls himself aboard.

- Others follow Abselseth to Collapsible A. They include passengers R. Norris Williams Jr. and Mrs. Rosa Abbott (the only woman to go down with the *Titanic* and survive), and crew members Fireman John Thompson and Steward Edward Brown.

- Lifeboat Collapsible B, which has washed off the *Titanic* upside down, is mobbed by a group of survivors. The cry of "Save one life! Save one life!" is reportedly heard by passengers in the boat. Among those hauling themselves aboard are Wireless Operator Harold Bride, who was hanging on for dear life underneath the boat, Second Officer Lightoller, and passengers John Thayer, A. K. Barkworth, and Colonel Archibald Gracie.

- Eventually 30 people are on Collapsible B, which begins to sink under the weight. At this point those on the boat begin attempting to keep others from getting on. Steward Thomas Whiteley and Fireman Harry Senior later recall being beaten with oars as they try to climb aboard. Eventually those on board begin to paddle away from the swimmers.

- Shortly after leaving the *Titanic* on Lifeboat No. 14, Fifth Officer Lowe takes command of a whole flotilla of boats, tying Nos. 14, 10, 12, 4, and Collapsible D together and dividing the total of 55 passengers among four of the boats. Hearing the screams in the water, Lowe and a handful of volunteers take boat 14 back to look for survivors. In an hour of searching, Lowe's boat plucks four survivors out of the icy water. One of those, W. F. Hoyt, will die an hour later of exposure.

- Third Officer Pitman, in boat No. 5, also hears the screams and starts to go back for survivors. But the protests of others on board force him to change his mind. Boat No. 5 has room for another 25 people.

- In boat No. 2 the question of whether to row back for survivors is put to a vote by Fourth Officer Boxhall. Those in the boat, which is only two-thirds full, vote no.

- In boat No. 6 the passengers are more than willing to go back for survivors. Quartermaster Hitchins refuses. Boat No. 6, capacity 65, has only 28 people in it.

- The opposite is the case in boat No. 1 when Fireman Charles Hendrickson yells "that it is up to us to go back." One passenger, Sir Cosmo Duff Gordon, speaks for the rest of the passengers when he suggests that going back might not be a good idea. Lifeboat No. 1, with only 12 people in a boat built for 40, stays put.

- Boat No. 14 will be the only boat to go back for survivors.

- Of the nearly 1,600 people who go down with the *Titanic*, only 13 are picked up by a total of 18 boats. Boat No. 4 rescues eight survivors who are nearby but does not go back.

- Fourth Officer Boxhall in boat No. 2 begins firing green flares in hopes of catching the attention of rescue ships. There is no response.

- The 18 lifeboats are spread out over a five-mile radius surrounding the area where the *Titanic* sank.

- Boats Nos. 5 and 7 tie up together, as do boats Nos. 6 and 16.

- At one point during the night a request is made by boat 6 to 16 to borrow an extra person to help row. Boat 16 complies.

- Lawrence Beesley attempts to tuck a blanket under the feet of a crying baby and discovers that the mother of the baby and he have mutual friends in England.

- Edith Russell offers another baby her toy pig to play with.

- Passenger Hugh Woolner feeds cookies to one of the kidnapped Navatril children.

- Mrs. John Jacob Astor loans a woman her shawl to cover her child.

- Marguerite Frolicher's seasickness is cured by a shot of brandy offered by another passenger.

- In boat No. 5 Third Officer Pitman wraps a sail around a very cold and shivering Mrs. Crosby.

- In boat No. 6 a freezing crewman is wrapped up in a fur coat offered by passenger Mrs. Brown.

- Charlotte Collyer, in boat No. 14, topples over from the cold. Her hair catches in one of the oarlocks and comes out by the roots when she attempts to right herself.

- In boat No. 13, Fireman Beauchamp, despite freezing from the cold, refuses the offer of a coat. He insists the woman offering the coat give it to a young girl instead.

- Mrs. John Thayer, in boat No. 4, rows for five hours straight.

- Seaman Jones later commented on the Countess of Rothes's behavior in boat No. 8, "I knew she was more of a man than any we had on board."

- Mrs. Charles Hayes, in boat No. 3, hails passing boats in search of her husband.

- In boat No. 8 Signora de Satode Penasco screams in vain for her husband Victor.

- Madame de Villiers, in boat No. 6, constantly calls for her son. Her son was not a passenger on the *Titanic*.

- Mrs. Washington Dodge, in boat No. 5, becomes so annoyed with her fellow passengers that when boat No. 7 comes by she jumps to that boat.

- An alarm clock keeps going off in boat No. 11.

- An argument breaks out in boat No. 3 when two *Titanic* crewmen light up cigarettes.

- C. E. Henry Stengel alienates himself from the rest of the people in boat No. 1 by constantly shouting "Boat ahoy!" and complaining about the way Lookout Symons is steering.

- A passenger hauled aboard boat No. 4 is found to be drunk. A bottle of brandy is taken off his person and thrown overboard. The drunk man is then roughly tossed into the bottom of the boat.

- An argument over who is in charge breaks out between Quartermaster Hitchens and Major Peuchen in boat No. 6. The argument later spills over into a confrontation between Hitchens and the women passengers who are doing most of the rowing. Hitchens, later that evening, has an emotional breakdown and Mrs. Brown becomes the unofficial commander of boat No. 6.

• An argument breaks out on the still upside down Collapsible B between Colonel Gracie and an unidentified man over the latter's dry outing cap. The argument is interrupted by the discovery that air is leaking out of Collapsible B and that the boat is sinking lower and lower into the water.

• Second Officer Lightoller attempts to counteract the sinking of the boat by having the men stand up in it and lean to the left and right. This ploy temporarily rights the boat.

• The legend of Captain Smith begins this night on boat No. 6. Assistant Cook John Maynard later recalls that Captain Smith climbed on his boat just as the *Titanic* went down but slipped off moments later. Fireman Harry Senior claims that Captain Smith let go on purpose, saying, "I will follow the ship!" Neither story will ever be totally proved or disproved.

• Passenger Walter Hurst takes a big swig of what he thinks is brandy and chokes. The liquid turns out to be essence of peppermint.

• Lightoller in Collapsible B discovers Wireless Operator Harold Bride at the other end of the boat and asks him what rescue ships he thinks are coming. Bride replies, the *Baltic*, the *Olympic,* and the *Carpathia.*

• Later that night a breeze springs up and the sea becomes suddenly choppy. Three men from Collapsible B slip off into the water and disappear.

• A miracle! Four hours after jumping overboard, Chief Baker Charles Joughin swims up to Collapsible B and is pulled aboard. Joughin had managed to survive those hours in freezing waters by drinking whiskey just before the ship went down.

CHAPTER 7

CARPATHIA
TO THE RESCUE

arpathia Captain Arthur H. Rostron was cut from a classic seafaring mold. He had boundless energy, made quick, insightful decisions, and had the respect of the crews that served under him. Captain Rostron's nickname was "the Electric Spark." It was a name given him by the Cunard shipping lines when he joined their company and steadily moved up the ranks to captain. It was in the position of captain of the *Lusitania* that Rostron honed those skills. Trust was a big thing to Rostron. So was respect. He had gained both by his ability to think fast.

In January 1912, Rostron was given command of the *Carpathia*. For Rostron, it was the high point of a career that had spanned nearly 20 years. On the night of April 14, the *Carpathia* was three days out of New York, hauling passengers and cargo on a leisurely run across the North Atlantic. The ship, carrying 725 passengers, would make stops in Genoa, Naples, Trieste, Fiume, and Gibraltar. It had been a rather uneventful, pleasantly warm day and so, after making one final, informal tour of the ship and handing off the watch to First Officer Dean, Rostron retired for the night.

- April 15. 12:35 A.M. Wireless Operator Harold Cottam bursts into Captain Rostron's quarters with the news that the *Titanic* has struck an iceberg and needs help.

- Rostron, once he has verified the urgency of the situation, orders Operator Cottam to tell the *Titanic,* "We are coming along as fast as we can."

- Rostron quickly determines that the *Carpathia* is 58 miles away from the *Titanic* and to the northwest. He immediately turns the *Carpathia* around and points it on a new course, North 52 West, directly for the *Titanic.*

- The *Carpathia*'s maximum speed is 14 knots. At that speed it will take the ship four hours to reach the *Titanic.* Rostron sends for Chief Engineer Johnstone and tells him to put every ounce of steam into the boilers.

- Rumors begin spreading among *Carpathia* passengers that their ship is on fire. Those rumors are quickly quashed by the news that the *Titanic* is in trouble.

- By 1 A.M. the *Carpathia* is speeding toward the *Titanic* at the unheard-of speed of 17 knots.

- The *Carpathia* continues to receive messages either directly or indirectly from the *Titanic.* At 1:06 A.M.

Wireless Operator Cottam hears, "Get your boats ready ... going down fast at the head." At 1:10 A.M. he hears, "Sinking head down." At 1:35 A.M. the *Titanic* reports, "Engine room getting flooded."

• The *Carpathia* receives its final message from the *Titanic* at 1:50 A.M. "Come as quickly as possible old man. The engine room is filling up to the boilers."

• 2:00 A.M. Captain Rostron realizes that the *Carpathia*, as it steams ahead at top speed, is also in danger of striking an iceberg. At that moment the only lookout is one man in the crow's nest. He orders a second man to the crow's nest, two men on the bow, and a man on each wing of the bridge.

• 2:40 A.M. Captain Rostron spots a green flare over the horizon and assumes that the *Titanic* is still afloat.

• 2:45 A.M. Captain Rostron orders the *Carpathia*'s signal rockets to be fired every 15 minutes to reassure the *Titanic* that she was in the vicinity "and running hard."

• 2:45 A.M. Second Officer James Bisset spots the first iceberg, a mile ahead.

• 2:45 A.M. to 3:30 A.M. The *Carpathia* continues full speed into the ice floes. During this period it will come close to but not strike five icebergs.

• At 3:30 A.M. The *Carpathia* fires off yet another round of signal rockets.

- 3:30 A.M. In boat No. 6 one passenger mistakes the rocket for a flash of lightning. Quartermaster Hitchens dismisses it as a falling star.

- In boat No. 13, a crewman, lying almost unconscious at the bottom of the boat, sits bolt upright and shouts out that he thinks he heard a cannon.

- In boat No. 9 a crewman calls for prayer.

- In boat No. 3 small fires are set with newspapers and a passenger's straw hat to signal back to the oncoming ship. In boat No. 13 they twist a torch out of letters. In boat No. 2, crewman Boxhall lights his last flare.

- 4 A.M. The *Carpathia* reaches the *Titanic*'s last known position. Total running time to the location: $3^1/_2$ hours. Rostron's decision to test the *Carpathia*'s engines has shaved 30 minutes off the estimated time of arrival.

- Rostron scans the horizon for the *Titanic* but sees nothing. Then he spots the blink of a green flare. 400 yards away bobs lifeboat No. 2.

- 4:05 A.M. The *Carpathia* starts toward boat No. 2 but suddenly slams to a halt. An iceberg stands dead ahead. Rostron immediately, cautiously, maneuvers the *Carpathia* to one side and past.

- 4:10 A.M. Lifeboat No. 2 is the first boat to be picked up by the *Carpathia*.

- The Collapsible B, still losing air, is four miles away when the *Carpathia* arrives.

- As the *Carpathia*'s lights flash out across the sea, Officer Lightoller spots boats 4, 8, 12, and Collapsible D 800 yards away. Lightoller takes out his officer's whistle and blows it.

- Seaman Frederick Clinch in boat No. 12 and crewman Samuel Hemming in boat No. 4 hear the whistle and spot Collapsible B off in the distance. The two boats immediately begin rowing toward Collapsible B.

- 4:45 A.M. Boat No. 13 reaches the *Carpathia*.

- 6:00 A.M. Boat No. 7 reaches the *Carpathia*, followed by most of the other boats.

- Boats No. 12 and 4 reach Collapsible B at approximately 6 A.M.

- Collapsible B passenger Jack Thayer is so intent on getting into boat No. 12 that he does not initially notice his mother sitting in lifeboat No. 4.

- Officer Lightoller, the last person to leave Collapsible B, lifts a dead body into No. 12 and then jumps in.

- 6:30 A.M. Having rescued the Collapsible B passengers, boats 12 and 4 begin rowing toward the *Carpathia*.

- 6:30 A.M. Lifeboats No. 12 and Collapsible D have

begun rowing toward the *Carpathia*. Boat D is riding low in the water and has few people rowing. Boat No. 14 pulls up, ties a line to the boat, and tows them for a mile and a half. En route to the *Carpathia*, they come upon Collapsible A.

• Collapsible A is in jeopardy. Of the 30 people on board at the time the *Titanic* sank, all but 13 have fallen overboard. Boat No. 14 pulls up and takes them aboard, and abandons A and three dead bodies that lie inside.

• 8:15 A.M. All the *Titanic*'s lifeboats have been picked up except No. 12, which is still several hundred yards away and now contains 75 people.

• 8:15 A.M. Colonel Gracie, in boat No. 12, attempts to revive a lifeless body. He fails in his attempts.

• 8:20 A.M. Boat No. 12 is now 200 yards away. Captain Rostron, in an attempt to shorten the distance, turns the *Carpathia*'s bow to within 100 yards of the lifeboat.

• 8:30 A.M. Lifeboat No. 12 reaches the *Carpathia* and its passengers are brought aboard.

• Rostron decides to take the *Titanic* survivors back to New York.

• *Titanic*'s sister ship *Olympic* arrives on the scene and offers to take the *Titanic* survivors. Rostron rejects the offer.

- 8:30 A.M. The *Carpathia* cruises through the area one last time in search of possible survivors. They find one body floating in the water.

- 8:50 A.M. Reverend Father Anderson leads a memorial service for the *Titanic* dead in the main lounge of the *Carpathia*.

- 8:50 A.M. The *Carpathia* turns and heads for New York.

- A storm batters the *Carpathia* on the way to New York and many *Titanic* survivors panic, thinking this ship, too, has struck an iceberg.

- The *Carpathia* physician indicates Norris Williams's badly frozen legs might have to be amputated. Williams refuses and begins a regular regime of walking. The circulation eventually returns to his legs.

- The survivors are finally informed that the *Titanic* had, in fact, received a number of warnings of ice ahead but had not slowed down.

CHAPTER 8

THE *CALIFORNIAN* MYSTERY

The *Californian* arrived at the site of the *Titanic* disaster at 8:30 A.M. and found itself with little to do. The *Carpathia* had already picked up the last of the survivors and was making ready for the voyage back to New York when *Californian* Captain Stanley Lord was patched through to Captain Rostron. Their conversation was quick and to the point. Lord offered to sweep the area one last time for survivors and Rostron said that would be fine.

Lord was feeling guilty. He had been in a position to be a real hero, but he had thrown away his chance and the fates had dealt him another hand. Lord's sadness would eventually turn to anger and then to blame.

The *Californian* had been only 19 miles away when the *Titanic* struck the iceberg at 11:40 A.M. That it had taken nearly nine hours for the *Californian* to arrive on the scene was an enigma Rostron would ponder at length in later years, as would historians and laymen alike. That many more lives would have been saved if the *Californian* had been the first on the scene went without question. That it was not made the *Titanic* disaster all the more tragic.

The *Californian*, a cargo ship carrying no passengers, had been on the much traveled Liverpool-to-Boston run. On April 14, at 10:21 P.M., she unexpectedly sailed right into the middle of an ice field. Captain Lord, who had a reputation for being cautious at the helm, decided to stop ship rather than risk a collision in the dark. Lord ordered the *Californian* engines put on standby, left the ship in charge of Third Officer Charles V. Groves, and went to his cabin.

Around 11 A.M., Groves spotted an unidentified steamer coming up from the southeast. Captain Lord was alerted that another ship was in the area. He asked Wireless Operator Cyril Evans what it might be and was informed that the *Titanic* was the only ship reported within hailing distance. Lord ordered Evans to hail the *Titanic* and warn them that there was ice ahead and that his ship was, in fact, surrounded. It was at that point that the *Californian* received the infamous "Shut up! I'm busy!" response from the *Titanic*.

• April 14. 11:45 P.M. Lord and Groves attempt to figure out the identity of the mystery ship. Groves feels the ship is, in fact, a passenger vessel and that it is no more than 10 miles away. Lord thinks it is a freighter and that it is merely five miles away. Groves continues trying to contact the ship as Captain Lord returns to his quarters.

• 12:00 midnight. Groves hands over the watch to Second Officer Herbert Stone. Captain Lord, as he prepares to retire for the night, advises Stone to let him know if the mystery ship gets any closer.

• April 15. 12:15 A.M. Groves goes to the wireless room. A budding wireless operator, he would often stop by and play around with the equipment. Wireless Operator Evans is getting ready to go off duty and was not in the wireless room when Groves begins to tinker with the set. Unfamiliar as he is with the equipment, he cannot make the receiver work. While he plays with the wireless equipment, the *Californian* is missing the *Titanic*'s first call for help.

• 12:15 A.M. to 12:45 A.M. Second Officer Stone, on the bridge, is keeping watch on the mystery ship. His initial impression is that the ship is a tramp steamer and not a passenger ship.

• 12:45 A.M. Second Officer Stone is startled by a series of rocket flashes bursting over the mystery ship. Stone rings up Captain Lord, who orders him to try once again to raise the ship by way of Morse lamp.

• 12:50 A.M. Stone is joined in the wireless room by Apprentice James Gibson. Gibson goes to the Morse lamp and signals for a total of three minutes. There is no response from the mystery ship. Another rocket flashes across the sky.

- 12:55 A.M. to 1:40 A.M. Stone and Gibson continue to watch the ship. Two more rockets are fired. At one point Gibson, watching through binoculars, suggests to Stone that the ship is listing to starboard. Both lookouts speculate, at the time, that the ship is actually sailing away from them.

- 2:00 A.M. Gibson awakens Captain Lord with the report that the ship has fired a number of rockets and that it now appears to be sailing away. Lord questions Gibson as to the color of the rockets. Gibson replies white.

- 2:05 A.M. to 2:40 A.M. Stone and Gibson continue to watch the ship until it completely disappears.

- 2:40 A.M. Stone once again reports to Captain Lord that the ship has, in fact, now disappeared completely from view and that they have spotted no further rockets. Lord once again wants to know the color of the rockets Stone saw. Stone once again says white.

- 2:40 A.M. to 3:20 A.M. Stone and Gibson continue their watch.

- 3:20 A.M. Stone and Gibson spot three more rocket flashes out on the horizon. Strangely, Stone does not report these flashes to Captain Lord.

- 4 A.M. The *Californian*'s chief officer, George F. Stewart, comes on the bridge to take over the watch. Stone reports to Stewart exactly what he observed and did on his watch. Stewart scans the horizon with his binoculars and spots a steamer that will later turn out to be the *Carpathia*. Stewart questions Stone as to whether this is the ship he had been observing in the previous hours. Stone replies no. Stone goes off watch, leaving Stewart with the uneasy feeling that something has possibly happened during the night and that they have not acted on it.

- 4:30 A.M. Captain Lord is awakened by Chief Stewart. He goes to the bridge and begins conferring with Stewart about how they are going to get out of the ice and continue their voyage to Boston. Stewart wants to know if Lord has any plans to find out more about the ship that was firing the rockets. Lord looks out at the *Carpathia* and mutters that "she looks all right now." Stewart does not tell Lord that he is looking at the wrong ship.

- 5:20 A.M. Chief Officer Stewart continues to be troubled by the previous night's events and finally wakes up Wireless Operator Evans with the request that he "find out what is wrong."

- 5:30 A.M. The *Californian* is advised by ships *Frankfort* and *Mount Temple* that the *Titanic* has, in fact, struck an iceberg and sunk.

- 5:45 A.M. The ship *Virginian* also confirms the story, giving the *Titanic*'s last known coordinates as 41° 16' N', 50° 14' W. The *Californian*'s coordinates are 42° 5'

N', 50° 7' W. To Captain Lord's horror, he finds that the *Titanic* was only 19 miles away when it went down.

• 6:00 A.M. Captain Lord has the *Californian* underway and heading toward the last known location of the *Titanic*.

• 6:00 A.M. to 7:00 A.M. The *Californian* zigzags its way through the first three or four miles of heavy ice and icebergs at a literal crawl. Once in open water, the ship increases its speed to 13 knots.

• 7:30 A.M. The *Californian* arrives at the posted coordinates but finds only the *Mount Temple* at the location. Lord eventually spots the *Carpathia* six miles to the east and heads for it.

• 8:30 A.M. The *Californian* arrives just as the *Carpathia* picks up lifeboat No. 12. It will stay in the area, searching for survivors, until 11:20 A.M. It finds no survivors and no bodies.

• The *Californian*'s log will not mention any of the rockets spotted the previous night and early morning.

• The *Californian* arrives in Boston on the morning of April 19. When questioned by reporters and agents for the shipping line, all its crew members deny having seen any rockets or lights on the night of April 14-15.

CHAPTER 9

THE MUSIC OF THE NIGHT

The musicians who sailed on the *Titanic* were all critically acclaimed and at the top of their profession. It is too bad that they boarded the *Titanic* as second-class citizens.

Prior to 1912, the steamship lines dealt directly with the musicians, treating them as crew members and paying them a decent union scale wage of 6 pounds 10 shillings a month plus a monthly uniform allowance of 10 shillings. Fairness went out the window with the coming of the Liverpool, England–based Black Talent Agency.

The agency immediately signed exclusive contracts with all the major steamship lines. Since Black was the only agency in town, musicians were forced to deal with them or not work. And dealing with Black meant a drastic cut in pay, to 4 pounds a month and no uniform allowance. Adding insult to injury, when the musicians' union approached J. Bruce Ismay regarding the matter, they promptly found themselves demoted from crew status to passenger class. And, as such, they were regu-

77

lated to cramped quarters on the E Deck next to the potato washer.

There was a total of eight musicians on the R.M.S. *Titanic* on her maiden voyage. But there were two distinct bands. The first group, a quintet, played background music during teatime and Sunday services and at after-dinner concerts. There was also a trio, consisting of a violin, cello, and piano player, whose main job was to play tunes with a decidedly French flavor, performing in the reception room outside the A la Carte Restaurant and Café Parisien.

The *Titanic*'s musicians had the reputation of being energetic in their presentation of hymns, waltzes and ragtime tunes. Their song list numbered 350, so the odds were good that audiences, whether on the deck of the Café Parisian or gathered in the saloon near the Grand Staircase, would always find something pleasing to listen or dance to.

And it was all eight musicians, playing as one unit, who picked up their instruments scant minutes after the *Titanic* struck the iceberg.

• The *Titanic* band began playing at 12:15 A.M. in the first-class lounge on the A Deck. Despite the seriousness of the moment, they were dressed in their regulation band uniforms with their green facings. They were not wearing lifejackets.

• As the night went on, the band moved up to the boat deck level of the Grand Staircase.

- They moved up to the boat deck proper at the end and played until the *Titanic* disappeared.

- At the start of the crisis, the band was instructed to play upbeat tunes to help calm down the passengers as they made for the lifeboats. The early portion of their song list included "Alexander's Ragtime Band" and "Great Big Beautiful Doll."

- The songs turned more patriotic as the tension mounted. That portion of their music list included "The Star Spangled Banner," "The Land of Hope," and "Londonderry Aire."

- In the final minutes, the band turned to hymns and music with a religious theme. The music included "When We Meet Beyond," "Lead, Kindly Light," "Abide with Me," and "Eternal Father, Strong to Save."

- The hymn "Nearer My God, to Thee" was, in fact, played.

- But the final piece of music played was "Songe d'Automne," a waltz by Archibald Joyce.

- After the *Titanic* sank, it was discovered that the band members were not covered by anybody's insurance policy. The White Star Line said that the band worked for the Black Talent Agency and therefore was covered by them. The Black Agency responded that, since the band were listed as passengers, they were covered by White Line's policy.

- On January 12, 1913, the *Titanic* Relief Fund, an organization in charge of contributions that had come in after the *Titanic* sank, announced that it would treat the musicians as members of the crew and pay their survivors accordingly.

- One sad final irony: On April 30, 1912, the family of violinist Jock Hume received a letter from the Black Talent Agency requesting the equivalent of $3.50 to cover his unpaid uniform bill.

The Titanic *rests at the Southampton dock, April 1912.*

*Captain Edward J. Smith
of the* Titanic.

The **Titanic** *steams out of Southampton on her maiden voyage shortly after noon on April 10, 1912.*

First-class passengers on the Titanic.

Passengers stroll along the second-class promenade on the boat deck.

The Turkish bath on the Titanic.

The reading room on the upper promenade deck.

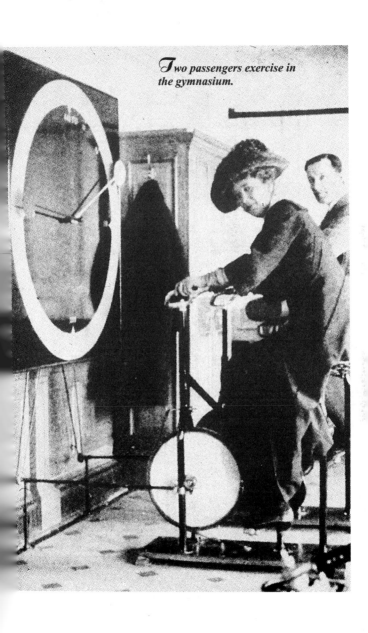

Two passengers exercise in the gymnasium.

WHITE STAR LINE
ROYAL ★ STEAMERS
UNITED STATES MAIL

FIRST SAILING OF THE LATEST ADDITION TO THE WHITE STAR FLEET

The Queen of the Ocean

TITANIC

LENGTH 882½ FT.   OVER 45,000 TONS   BEAM 92½ FT.
TRIPLE-SCREWS

This, the Latest, Largest and Finest Steamer Afloat, will sail from

WHITE STAR LINE, PIER 59 (North River), NEW YORK

Saturday, April 20th At 12 Noon

All passengers berthed in closed rooms containing 2, 4, or 6 berths, a large number equipped with washstands, etc.

THIRD CLASS FOUR BERTH ROOM
Spacious Dining Saloons
Smoking Room
Ladies' Reading Room
Covered Promenade

THIRD CLASS DINING SALOON

Reservations of Berths may be made direct with this Office or through any of our accredited Agents

THIRD CLASS RATES ARE:

To PLYMOUTH, SOUTHAMPTON, LONDON, LIVERPOOL and GLASGOW,	$36.25
To GOTHENBURG, MALMÖ, CHRISTIANIA, COPENHAGEN, ESBJERG, Etc.	41.50
To STOCKHOLM, ÅBO, HANGO, HELSINGFORS	44.50
To HAMBURG, BREMEN, ANTWERP, AMSTERDAM, ROTTERDAM, HAVRE, CHERBOURG	45.00

TURIN, $48.   NAPLES, $82.50.   PIRAEUS, $55.   BEYROUTH, $61, Etc, Etc.

DO NOT DELAY: Secure your tickets through the local Agents or direct from

WHITE STAR LINE, 9 Broadway, New York

TICKETS FOR SALE HERE

This White Star Line poster advertising the Titanic's *return trip from New York.*

There were an unprecedented number of icebergs in the steamship lanes of the North Atlantic in spring 1912. This berg, photographed from the deck of the rescue ship Mackay-Bennett, *may be the one that sank the* Titanic *on April 14.*

No.	Words.	Origin. Station.	Time handed in.			Via.	Remarks.
			H	M	10		
To		Titanic					

CQD°SOS cos cqd cqd — m gy

We are sinking fast passengers on being put into boats

m gy

One of the last distress calls sent out by First Wireless Officer John Phillips in the early morning hours of April 15.

Survivors are lifted aboard the Carpathia.

The headlines of The New York Times *on April 16, 1912 proclaim the horrific news.*

MR. JACK PHILLIPS, FIRST WIRELESS OPERATOR OF THE "TITANIC," WHOSE SIGNALS BROUGHT THE "CARPATHIA" TO THE SCENE OF THE DISASTER AND WHO DIED FROM EXPOSURE.
Photograph by Central News

MR. HAROLD BRIDE, SECOND WIRELESS OPERATOR, WHO WAS SAVED, AND IS REPORTED TO HAVE DEALT EFFECTIVELY WITH A MAN WHO TRIED TO TAKE PHILLIPS' LIFEBELT.
Photograph by Illustrations Bureau

MR. W. T. STEAD, THE FAMOUS JOURNALIST, WHO WENT DOWN WITH THE "TITANIC," BUT OF WHOSE END NOTHING IS DEFINITELY KNOWN.
Photograph News

MR. KARL H. BEHR, THE FAMOUS LAWN-TENNIS PLAYER, EX-CAPTAIN OF YALE, WHO WAS SAVED.
Photograph by Sport and General

MR. R. M. WILLIAMS, A MOST PROMISING AMERICAN LAWN-TENNIS PLAYER, WHO WAS SAVED.
Photograph by Sport and General

MAJOR A. W. BUTT, AIDE-DE-CAMP TO PRESIDENT TAFT, DROWNED AFTER HELPING MANY WOMEN AND CHILDREN TO THE BOATS.
Photograph by Illustrations Bureau

CAPTAIN E. J. SMITH, R.N.R., OF THE "TITANIC," WHO WENT TO A SEAMAN'S GRAVE WITH HIS SHIP, AFTER DOING ALL HE COULD TO SAVE THE WOMEN AND CHILDREN.
Photograph by Langfier, Illustrations

MR. ISIDOR STRAUS, THE AMERICAN MILLIONAIRE, WHOSE WIFE REFUSED TO LEAVE HIS SIDE AND PERISHED WITH HIM.
Photograph by Illustrations Bureau

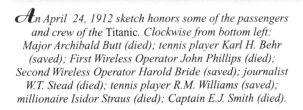

An April 24, 1912 sketch honors some of the passengers and crew of the Titanic. *Clockwise from bottom left: Major Archibald Butt (died); tennis player Karl H. Behr (saved); First Wireless Operator John Phillips (died); Second Wireless Operator Harold Bride (saved); journalist W.T. Stead (died); tennis player R.M. Williams (saved); millionaire Isidor Straus (died); Captain E.J. Smith (died).*

In recognition of his courage and resolution in "heroically saving seven-hundred-and-four passengers of the Titanic *mid-ocean," the Congress of the United States presented* Carpathia *captain Arthur Henry Rostron with this medal on July 6, 1912.*

After the the sinking of the Titanic, *a disaster fund was set up to collect money for families of the victims. Here British Boy Scouts solicit passersby.*

Mr. and Mrs. J. Bruce Ismay (right) en route to the British Board of Trade investigation into the sinking of the Titanic. Harold Sanderson, general manager of the White Star Line, is on the left.

Edmund and Michel Natravil pose with their mother after the Titanic *disaster. The boys had been abducted by their father, who boarded the* Titanic *under the name "Hoffman" and handed the boys over to passengers on the Collapsible D shortly before the ship sank. The children were later reunited with their mother in Nice.*

Survivor Katherine Manning, age 66, holds a prayer book and an I.D. card from the Titanic. *She was 16 years old and on her way from Dublin to a new life in America when the ship went down.*

Thirteen Titanic *lifeboats were brought aboard the* Carpathia *and returned to the White Star Line in New York.*

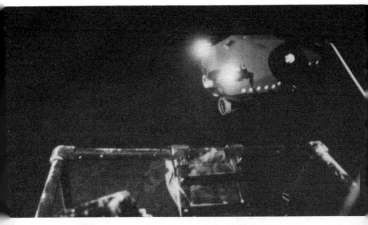

During Robert Ballard's 1986 expedition, the robotic vehicle Jason Jr. *leaves the manned submersible* Alvin *and sets out to photograph the wreck of the* Titanic.

Underwater cameras photographed two bollards used to secure mooring lines and a railing on the starboard side of the Titanic.

A remote-operated camera aboard the sunken Titanic *looks out at a piece of the ship's ribbing, a railing, and a porthole. The brass rim of the porthole has been kept polished by swift currents moving along the ocean floor.*

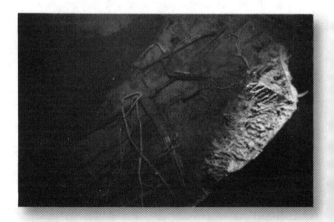

Debris litters a section of the hull of Titanic*'s stern, peeled outward by the force of the ship's destruction. Robert Ballard and his expedition found the stern a third of a mile south of the bow section.*

CHAPTER 10

TITANIC: THE AFTERMATH

*S*hortly after the *Carpathia* left the area with the *Titanic* survivors, J. Bruce Ismay wired the White Star Line offices with the following message:

"Deeply regret advise you *Titanic* sank this morning after collision with iceberg, resulting in serious loss of life. Full particulars later."

The rest of the world was just waking up, unaware, for the moment, of the latest *Titanic* news. Many were still savoring the news reels they had seen of the majestic ship on its maiden voyage. The more imaginative— and the wealthier—were making plans to book passage on a future voyage.

Ismay's message would be the first official news of the tragedy to reach the world. And it would be the last word from the *Carpathia* until the ship arrived in New York three days later. But it would not be the first word of the *Titanic* disaster to be released. At 1:20 A.M. on April 15, an Associated Press message went out announcing that the *Titanic* had struck an iceberg and

81

had sent out messages to all ships requesting help. Only a handful of papers ran with this skeletal information in their morning editions.

But it was enough to set off a stampede of reporters to the White Star Lines offices in New York. When the company's Vice-President, P. A. S. Franklin, arrived at the office at 8 A.M., Franklin, with no concrete information, steadfastly announced that "We believe that the boat is unsinkable." Similar words were offered in the hours that followed, as friends and relatives of *Titanic* passengers poured into the White Star offices—despite the fact that White Star, by this time, had received Ismay's message.

Franklin and the rest of the White Star executives were in a quandary. How should they break the news that would almost certainly change the face of the White Star Line forever? Franklin justified keeping things close to the vest by reasoning that the news, while horrifying, had been sketchy at best. It would be best not to say anything until he had the whole story. The truth was not long in coming.

At 6:15 P.M. a message from the ship *Olympic* offered the real story of the *Titanic*'s sinking, the survivors, and the *Carpathia*'s role in the rescue. As papers were going to press with this news in their late editions on April 15, White Star continued to deny the fact that the *Titanic* had gone down. Finally, at 7 P.M., with reporters littering his waiting room, Franklin, who had worn a path on his office carpet and was repeatedly wiping the sweat from his brow, came out with the first official White Star admission of what really happened to the *Titanic*.

"I regret to say that the *Titanic* sank at 2:20 this morning."

Franklin was tight-lipped after that, but he started to crack within the hour. When confronted once again by reporters at 8 P.M., he stated that the *Olympic* message had neglected to say that all the crew had been saved. By 8:15, his tune had changed to "Probably a number of lives have been lost." By 8:45, the message was "We very much fear that there has been a great loss of life." Franklin finally caved in at 9 P.M. and admitted that there had been "a horrible loss of life."

By 11 P.M. that night, the first list of survivors had been posted in the White Star Line office—which succeeded only in adding to the general confusion, relief, and anguish.

With as yet no formal survivor list, notification of next of kin was haphazard at best. Reporters, who at this point were sniffing up a storm around the incident, had tracked down relatives and were placing insensitive calls, asking them their opinion of the tragedy and trying to elicit an emotional reaction. The response was predictable: frantic calls to the White Star Line and a surge of panic and terror.

• April 17. The White Star Line, under pressure from the press, attempts to put their best foot forward and hires the ship *Mackay-Bennett*, out of Halifax, Canada, to race to the disaster site to search for bodies.

• April 17. 12 noon. U.S. Senator William Alden Smith directs the Committee on Commerce to name a subcommittee to investigate the *Titanic* disaster. Senator Smith is named to head up the investigation.

• April 17. A message from the *Carpathia* to the U.S. White Star offices is intercepted by the U.S. cruiser *Chester*. The message, not too subtly, asks that space for all of the British *Titanic* survivors be saved on the ship *Cedric*. The obvious intent of the message, signed "Yamsi," is to get British subjects away from any legal inquiries. "Yamsi" spelled backward is "Ismay." Senator Smith, his subcommittee members, and an army of marshals immediately leave for New York.

• April 18. 8:00 P.M. The *Carpathia* arrives in New York. More than 10,000 people stand on the shore watching as it steams past the Statue of Liberty. The *Carpathia* is originally set to dock at Cunard Lines pier No. 54. But when Captain Rostron sees an estimated 30,000 people there, including an unknown number of reporters, he keeps going up the river until he reaches the White Star piers.

• 8:37 P.M. The *Carpathia* docks at the White Star piers and the thirteen *Titanic* lifeboats that have been brought aboard are dropped off.

- 9:35 P.M. The *Carpathia* returns to the Cunard pier. As the gangplank falls, the first people on the boat, before anyone leaves, are Senator Smith and his marshals. They go straight to the chief surgeon's cabin, where they find J. Bruce Ismay. Senator Smith informs Ismay that a subcommittee has been convened to investigate the *Titanic* disaster. Ismay says he will cooperate in any way he can.

- 9:40 P.M. The first *Titanic* survivors step off the *Carpathia* and are immediately mobbed by family, friends, and reporters. The latter group, in many cases, wave 50-dollar bills in the air as an inducement to survivors to talk.

- April 19. 10:00 A.M. The U.S. subcommittee convenes in the east room of the Waldorf-Astoria Hotel.

- April 19. 10:30 A.M. Senator Smith offically opens the hearings and calls J. Bruce Ismay as the first witness. Ismay's testimony will total 58 pages.

- April 19 to May 25. A total of 82 witnesses, 20 of them passengers, give testimony during the U.S. hearings.

- April 22. The *Mackay-Bennett* reports to the White Star Line that, in six days, it has found 306 bodies at the *Titanic* site. One of those is the body of John Jacob Astor, which was badly mangled when one of the *Titanic*'s huge funnels fell down on him. A second boat, the *Minia*, is sent out to help look for bodies.

- April 24. The *Titanic*'s sister ship, *Olympic*, is about to depart from Southampton, England, when its crew rebels, stating they will not work on a ship that does not carry enough lifeboats. White Star refuses to add more boats. 285 crewmen desert. The *Olympic*'s voyage is canceled.

- April 29. The *Minia* reports finding another 17 bodies at the *Titanic* site.

- May 2. The British government, irritated at the U.S. subcommittee hearings, convenes a British Board of Trade special court to investigate the tragedy. Lord Mersey is selected to head up the special court.

- May 2 to July 3. The British Board of Trade court will ask 96 witnesses a total of 25,622 questions.

- May 6. The White Star Line sends out another ship, the *Montmagny*, to help search for bodies. It recovers 4 bodies.

- May 13. The White Star Line ship *Oceanic*, on a regularly scheduled run across the North Atlantic, spots *Titanic* lifeboat Collapsible A bobbing in the waves approximately 230 miles from where the *Titanic* went down. Inside were three bodies that were abandoned when the passengers climbed on the *Carpathia*. The three bodies are sewn up in canvas bags and buried at sea. The Collapsible A is sunk.

- May 15. One more ship, the *Algerina*, is sent to search

for bodies. It recovers only one body. The White Star-commissioned ships find a total of 328 bodies.

• May 25. The U.S. inquiry ends. The conclusions: The *Titanic* was going too fast. A good and proper lookout was not kept. There was poor organization in loading and lowering the lifeboats. The *Californian* saw the *Titanic*'s distress rockets and could have come to its aid. The inquiry also determines that there was no discrimination against third-class passengers.

• June 1912. The *Ilford*, a steamer en route from Galveston to Hamburg, picks up the badly decomposed body of *Titanic* crew member W .F. Cheverton. They bury him at sea.

• July 3. The British Board of Trade special court agrees with all the U.S. findings, adding the following recommendations: Passenger ships should carry enough lifeboats for all aboard. There should be better and more frequent lifeboat drills. Wireless operators should be on duty 24 hours a day. The quality of watertight compartments should be improved.

• In the aftermath of the *Titanic* tragedy, a total of $16 million in claims is filed for loss of life and property. The highest amount, $1,000,000, is filed by the widow of Broadway theater owner and producer Henry B. Harris. Surviving relatives of the Astors, Wideners, Guggenheims, and Strauses file no claims. Their feeling is that it is too demeaning to put a price on a human life.

• Through a loophole in American maritime law, in which lawsuits are determined by the total value of everthing salvaged from the ship plus the money paid by passengers and shippers, the White Star Line's lawyers finally come up with a more manageable amount of $97,772.12.

• October 8. The White Star Line petitions the U.S. Federal District Court for limited liability under American law. The District Court finds for the White Star Line, but the decision is appealed. The U.S. Supreme Court ultimately finds in favor of White Star. Claimants on both sides of the Atlantic protest the decision.

• June 22, 1915. The case against the White Star Line on behalf of the survivors of the *Titanic* victims comes to trial in England.

• July 27–29, 1915. Final arguments are heard by Judge Julius M. Mayer. He examines the case and the evidence presented. Mayer has a reputation for being detail oriented, and so both sides expect months of delay before a final determination is made.

• In the meantime, lawyers from both sides confer. White Star begins offering increasingly larger amounts to settle, while the claimants begin scaling down their demands.

- On December 17, 1915. White Star announces that it has agreed to pay a total of $664,000 to be split up among the claimants.

- July 28, 1916. The settlement is formally signed and sealed after a total of four years, three months, one week and six days of litigation.

CHAPTER 11

LIFE AFTER *TITANIC*

On April 21, 1912, a rumor began circulating that J. Bruce Ismay, unable to stand the strain of the *Titanic* disaster and its aftermath, had committed suicide in New York. Ismay surfaced, very much alive, but the rumor was a foreshadowing of the life he would lead in the years after *Titanic*.

If Ismay had, in fact, killed himself, it would almost have been an understandable act. In the wake of the disaster, Ismay had become a symbol of everything that went wrong. It was his ship, so it should have been built to withstand the terrors of the sea. He survived because he was upper crust, while those in steerage were allowed to perish. In the days and months that followed, his strong, determined stride deteriorated into a weak shuffle. He would take great pains to avoid going out in public. And then there were the U.S. and British inquiries to be endured.

The U.S. inquiry was a particularly brutal process. Ismay was grilled mercilessly. Questions were asked and asked again. Accusations, veiled and not so veiled, were made. And sitting in the inquiry room was a horde of reporters, quick to take notes and mold the information to their own liking. A scapegoat was needed and, with Captain Smith dead, the mantle fell on Ismay's unfortunate shoulders.

The British inquiry, by comparison, was a bit more gentle but, in the end, Ismay was once again the target; his interpretation of the facts and his memories of what happened that night were questioned. In a way, the British admonition of Ismay was a much more painful cross to bear than what he had endured in the States.

Although the British Board of Trade special court would ultimately clear Ismay of any moral obligation to stay with the sinking ship, the popular opinion held that Ismay had behaved in a cowardly manner on that night and should have stayed with the ship until the bitter end. The newly formed town of Ismay, Texas, immediately changed its name to something less infamous. The much braver citizenry of Ismay, Montana, hung on to the namesake.

Ismay had every intention of staying on as chairman of the White Star Line, but the bad press surrounding his actions on the *Titanic* soon rattled the company's corporate offices and, on June 30, 1913, he was—depending on your level of cynicism—either forced out or voluntarily retired as chairman. He would remain on a number of White Star boards, but these were purely honorary positions in which he wielded no real power or influence.

Shortly thereafter, Ismay retired from public life to

his estate in Northern Ireland. From then on, he rarely appeared in public. J. Bruce Ismay died of a stroke at his home in London on October 17, 1937.

Ismay's post-*Titanic* life was typical of the rocky personal and professional lives that dogged the survivors. Not all ended in suicide, but the trials and tribulations of first-class passengers Mr. and Mrs. Bill Carter were an example of the suffering survivors of the disaster experienced.

In January 1914, Mrs. Carter sued Bill Carter for divorce on the grounds of "cruel and barbarous treatment and indignities to the person." Further investigation revealed that the charges stemmed from the night the *Titanic* went down. After making sure his wife and children were safely on lifeboat No. 4, Bill Carter made a run for Collapsible C. Owing to the chaos of that night, Collapsible C ended up leaving the *Titanic* 15 minutes before No. 4. Mrs. Carter took this perceived breach of their marriage vows as a sign that their relationship was over. A judge agreed and granted the divorce.

Rather quickly, Mrs. Carter remarried one George Brooke and lived an uneventful life until her death in 1934. Bill Carter, an inveterate club hopper and polo player, continued both occupations until his death in 1940.

Other survivors had their stories:

• Renee Harris, Mrs. Astor, Mrs. Widener, and Mrs. Ryerson were among the women widowed on the *Titanic* who later remarried.

- Mrs. Lucien P. Smith remarried fellow *Titanic* survivor Robert Daniel.

- *Titanic* survivor Karl Behr married *Titanic* survivor Helen Newsom in March 1913. Behr was a top-ranked tennis player until 1915. He would subsequently sit on the board of many corporations, including Goodyear Tire and Rubber and National Cash Register. After Behr's death in 1949, Helen married Dean Mathey, another tennis player and a good friend of her late husband. Helen died in New Jersey in 1965.

- Cardshark George Brayton picked up where he left off and was deep into a card game on the *Carpathia*.

- William Sloper, who left in the first boat off the *Titanic*, was later accused by a spiteful reporter of dressing in women's clothes to get off the ship. Sloper would spend the rest of his life explaining the truth of the matter.

- Sir Cosmo Duff Gordon also fell under a cloud when charges were made that he had paid each of the crewmen on boat No. 1 five pounds each not to go back and pick up survivors in the water. He would spend years ignoring the charges before his death in 1931.

- His wife, Lady Lucy Duff Gordon, was a topflight dress designer before the *Titanic* incident and remained so until 1934, when her business empire collapsed. She died broke in April 1935.

- Mrs. Henry B. Harris went on to have a full and productive life, first as the first woman Broadway theater producer and then as a producer of troop shows during World War I. She would marry four more times but would maintain the Harris name. She died in September 1969 at the age of 93.

- Helen Churchill Candee continued to write, lecture, and travel. She died at age 90 in her home in York Harbor, Maine.

- Twelve-year-old Ruth Becker returned to a normal life in Ohio. After college she married Daniel Blanchard and divorced him 20 years later. During this period she taught high school in Kansas. After retirement she moved to Santa Barbara, California. In March 1990 she went on her first sea cruise since the *Titanic*. She died that same year at the age of 90.

- Richard Becker, Ruth's younger brother, was two years old when the *Titanic* went down. He had a career as a singer and, later, as a social welfare worker. He married twice and was widowed both times. He died in 1975.

- Four-year-old Marion Becker survived the *Titanic* but contracted tuberculosis at a young age and died in Glendale, California in 1944.

- Nellie Becker, the children's mother, was taking her children to the United States on the *Titanic* to get Richard treatment for an illness he had contracted in

India with his missionary father. The *Titanic* incident scarred her emotionally. In later years she was given to emotional outbursts and could never discuss the *Titanic* without breaking down. She died in 1961.

• Richard and Sally Beckwith went on to live normal, uneventful lives. Richard died in 1933, Sally in 1955.

• Joseph Boxhall, the *Titanic*'s fourth officer, continued with the White Star Line after its subsequent merger with Cunard. He served as chief officer on the ship *Ausonia*. He eventually left White Star and served with the Royal Navy before retiring from sea service in 1940. In 1958 he served as technical advisor on the *Titanic* film *A Night to Remember*. Boxhall died in 1967, and his ashes were scattered over the *Titanic* sinking site.

• Wireless Operator Harold Bride served in the same capacity on a steamer, *Mona's Isle*, during World War I. Following the war he became a salesman. He passed away in 1956.

• Fifth Officer Lowe became third officer on the Australian ship the *Medic*. He served in the Royal Navy during World War I before retiring in Wales.

• Third Officer Pitman transferred to the purser's section. For a time he served on board the *Titanic*'s sister ship *Olympic*. He retired to the town of Pitcombe, England, where he died in 1961.

- Second Officer Lightoller served in the Royal Navy in World War I. He returned to the White Star Line after the war and became chief officer on the *Celtic*. He eventually retired and spent his time writing newspaper columns and raising chickens. Eventually he designed his own yacht, the *Sundowner*, and, in 1940, became a hero when he sailed the *Sundowner* into the battle of Dunkirk and rescued 131 British soldiers.

- Fredrick Fleet, the lookout who spotted the iceberg, left sea service in 1936 but continued to work in the Harland and Wolff shipyards during World War II. In later years he would work as a night watchman for the Union Castle Line and sell newspapers . In 1965 Fleet, dispondent over financial problems and the recent loss of his wife, committed suicide.

- Japanese bureaucrat Masabumi Hosono jumped into a lifeboat as it was being lowered into the sea. This act of self-preservation subsequently branded him a coward in his native Japan. He was fired from his job and spent the rest of his days a broken, bitter man.

- Mrs. Rosa Abbott, the only woman to go down with the *Titanic* and live, moved to Rhode Island and became a seamstress. She remarried in 1914 and moved to Florida. Her whereabouts after 1928 are unknown.

- Madeleine Astor, who was left millions in the will of her husband, was remarried in 1919 to an elderly stockbroker named William Dick, who subsequently died.

Astor took a third husband, professional boxer Enzo Fiermonte, and seemed quite happy, but she committed suicide in 1937.

• Schoolteacher Lawrence Beesley returned to his profession and, in 1913, wrote a book about his experiences on the *Titanic*. Beesley died in 1967 at the age of 89.

• The three *Titanic* cardsharps wasted little time getting back to business. They reportedly swindled many *Titanic* survivors out of money totaling $30,000. Far less substantial is the report that one of the three was, years later, elected the mayor of New York City.

• After arriving in New York, third-class passenger Eva Hart was immediately deported. She would eventually wind up in Australia and have a long career as a singer. She would later become a British magistrate and would be honored by Queen Elizabeth for her charity work. In 1987 she protested the recovery of *Titanic* artifacts.

• Samuel Hemming testified at both the American and British inquiries regarding the *Titanic* disaster. He continued to work for the White Star Line until World War I.

• The famous *Titanic* kidnapped children, Edmund and Michel Navratil aka Hoffman, were returned to their mother in Nice. Edmund became an interior decorator, married, and served in the French army during

World War II, and was interned in a German prisoner-of-war camp. Edmund escaped the camp, but his health declined and he died at age 43. Michel became a professor of psychology and is still living in Paris.

• Edith Russell's toy pig, which she used to calm frightened children in her lifeboat, made a cameo appearance in the movie *A Night to Remember*. She died on April 4, 1975 at the age of 98.

• Mary Sloan was one of the last women off the *Titanic*. When the *Carpathia* arrived in New York, she disappeared and was never seen or heard from again.

• Olaus Abelseth returned to his South Dakota farm and raised cattle and sheep for the next 30 years. He died in North Dakota in 1980.

• Molly Brown, always a little rough around the edges, found herself accepted in polite society in the aftermath of the *Titanic* sinking. She was even considered a viable Congressional candidate for a while in 1914. She died of a stroke in 1932. After her death, she became the subject of a hit Broadway musical and film, *The Unsinkable Molly Brown*.

• Kate Buss married her fiancé, Samuel Willis, on May 11, 1912. The couple had one daughter. After her husband's death in 1953, Kate moved to Oregon to be with her daughter. She died there in 1972 at the age of 96.

- Colonel Archibald Gracie wrote the first serious book on the *Titanic* disaster, *The Truth About the Titanic*. He died on December 12, 1912, and his book was published after his death.

- Three-year-old Eugenie Baclini was the first *Titanic* survivor to die. He died of meningitis in August 1912.

- Esther Hart returned to England, where she died of cancer in 1928.

- Quartermaster Robert Hitchens, the man who steered the *Titanic* into the iceberg, eventually relocated to South Africa, where he became the harbor master in Cape Town.

- One of the saddest survivors of the *Titanic*, Marie Jerwan, would suffer from nightmares and panic attacks for some time after the incident. She would go on to battle cancer for years, be seriously injured in a 1974 auto accident, and die at the age of 86, after breaking her hip.

- Major Arthur Peuchen lived under a cloud of cowardice for years following the *Titanic* sinking for simply having survived. His military career in the Canadian army thrived. He was eventually promoted to the rank of lieutenant colonel of the Queen's Own Arms. He died in Alberta, Canada, in 1929.

- Emily Ryerson, who lost her husband and son in the *Titanic* disaster, worked with Herbert Hoover on behalf of the French wounded during World War I, for which she received the honor of Croix de Guerre from the French government. She met and married financial advisor Forsythe Sherfesee in 1927. She died in 1939 while vacationing in Uruguay.

• Elmer and Juliet Taylor were not fazed by their *Titanic* experience and continued to cross the Atlantic regularly, many times on the *Titanic*'s sister ship *Olympic*. Juliet Taylor died in 1927. Elmer would marry twice more before his death in 1949.

• Marian Thayer moved to Haverford, Pennsylvania where she lived until her death in 1944.

• Jack Thayer went on to the University of Pennsylvania and went into banking. The horror of the *Titanic* would continue to haunt him and, in 1945, he took his own life.

• Edwina Troutt moved to southern California where she married the first of her three husbands. She was one of a handful of *Titanic* survivors who would regularly talk about her experiences. She died in 1984 at the age of 100.

• Eleanor Widener devoted much of the rest of her life to charitable works. She passed away in Paris in 1937.

• Marion Wright lived a normal life after *Titanic*. She married Arthur Woolcott and moved to Cottage Grove, Oregon, where she raised three sons. She would rarely speak about the *Titanic* before her death in 1965.

- July 19, 1912. Captain Peter Pryal reported that he ran into the *Titanic*'s Captain Smith at the intersection of Baltimore and Paul Streets in Baltimore, Maryland. "There is no possibility of my being mistaken," he said. "I have known Captain Smith too long. I would know him even without his beard. I firmly believe that he was saved and, in some mysterious manner, has been brought to this country. I am willing to swear to my statement." Dr. Warfield, a local physician, reported that he had been treating Captain Pryal for some time and felt he was perfectly sane.

- Both Edward Ryan and Daniel Buckley would spend the rest of their lives denying eyewitness reports that they got on lifeboats dressed as women.

- Frank "Lucks" Towers, who later claimed to have survived the sinkings of both the *Lusitania* and the *Empress of Ireland*, surfaced with the report that he had served in the engine room crew of the *Titanic* and survived. Towers's name was not on the crew list, but he claimed he was traveling under an assumed name.

- *New York Times* reporter Jim Speers, who scored a *Titanic* scoop with his interview with crewman Harold Bride, shot to journalistic stardom on the strength of his *Titanic* coverage.

- Quartermaster George Rowe, who was the very last *Titanic* crew member to learn that the *Titanic* had struck an iceberg and was sinking, went on to serve in the British mercantile service during World War I and World War II. He retired in 1955.

• The *Californian* and its captain, Stanley Lord, would forever remain under a cloud for their failure to respond to the *Titanic*'s distress rockets and calls. Lord, who lost his command over the incident, died in 1962. The *Californian* was torpedoed and sunk during World War I.

• The *Carpathia* was torpedoed and sunk by a German submarine on July 17, 1918.

• Thirteen of the *Titanic*'s lifeboats were recovered by the *Carpathia* and returned to the White Star Line in New York. The word *Titanic* and the boats' numbers were removed, and the boats were shipped back to England, where they were placed, anonymously, on other White Star Line ships.

• The White Star Line merged with the Cunard Line, owner of the *Carpathia*, in 1934.

• The *Olympic*, the *Titanic*'s sister ship, was recalled and rebuilt in the wake of the *Titanic* sinking. In 1918 the *Olympic* collided with a German submarine and sank it. The ship was given the nickname of "Old Reliable." In 1934, the ship struck and sank a floating lighthouse. The *Olympic*'s captain was sued.

CHAPTER 12

IN SEARCH
OF THE *TITANIC*

*D*reams of raising the *Titanic* were not long in coming. Rumors of gold, diamonds, art masterpieces in watertight containers, and other reported riches fueled the imaginations of explorers and treasure hunters alike. One of the hottest rumors was that a cache of gold coins and bullion had been secretly stored on board by the British government and was being shipped to the United States as part of a deal with the American government.

But the challenges were many and daunting. The *Titanic* finally settled on the ocean floor at a depth of 13,000 feet, and despite its last coordinates being known, many speculated that shifting waters and the encroachment of water-driven silt would make discovering its exact location difficult, and that retrieving its cargo or, in wild speculation, actually raising the *Titanic* to the surface were pipe dreams.

The same year the *Titanic* went down, representatives of the Astor, Guggenheim, and Widener families were in contact with the Merritt and Chapman

Wrecking Company, talking seriously about the possibility of a salvage operation being undertaken at the *Titanic* site. That same year, an issue of the magazine *Popular Mechanics* ran an article that speculated that children just born when the *Titanic* went down would someday be able to see photographic images of the sunken ship.

In March, 1914, fewer than two years after that fateful night, a Denver, Colorado-based architect named Charles Smith concocted the first scheme to bring the mighty ship up from the depths. And the plan was nothing if not radical.

Smith's idea called for powerful electromagnets to be attached to a specially designed submarine. The *Titanic*'s steel hull would be attracted to the submarine's magnets, and thus the exact location of the ship would be fixed. Additional electromagnets would then be lowered and attached to the *Titanic*'s hull, and cables would be run from those magnets to winches on a number of barges situated on the surface. According to Smith, the winches would haul away and pull the *Titanic* to the surface.

Smith felt the feat could be accomplished with a total of 162 men at a cost of $1.5 million. A number of people felt there was a logic to Smith's plan. Unfortunately, nobody was willing to come up with the money and so Smith's plan was permanently retired. But the search for the *Titanic* had definitely begun.

• July 1953. The British salvage vessel *Help*, equipped

with explosives, deep-dive telephoto cameras and remote-control salvage gear, leaves Southampton, England, and heads for the last known position of the *Titanic*. The *Help*'s crew hope to blow open the *Titanic*'s hull and search for the rumored treasure. They never find the ship.

• The *Help* returns in July 1954. Once again nothing is found. The *Help* gives up and never returns.

• 1966. *Titanic* fanatic Douglas Woolley proposes a plan to find the *Titanic* by using a bathyscaphe. He further proposes attaching nylon balloons to its hull and pumping them full of air so that the ship rises to the surface. Skeptics want to know how Woolley plans on inflating the balloons at 13,000 feet below sea level.

• 1968. Two Hungarian inventors and a mysterious group of West German investors appropriate the essence of Woolley's idea. Their plan calls for plastic bags to be filled with hydrogen produced by electrolysis of the sea water. It is estimated that 85,000 cubic yards of hydrogen would be needed to raise the ship. The project, dubbed the *Titanic* Salvage Company, falls apart when the money fails to materialize and a chemistry professor provides the facts and figures that indicate it would take ten years to fill the balloons.

• During the 1970s, a number of radical ideas are

floated as to how to raise the *Titanic*. They include:

Pumping into the hull 180,000 tons of molten wax, which, when hardened, would become buoyant and lift the *Titanic* to the surface.

Pumping in Vaseline which would, likewise, harden and become buoyant.

Injecting thousands of Ping-Pong balls into the hull.

Giant winches to crank the ship up.

Encasing the *Titanic* in ice, which would then rise to the surface.

Using of millions of glass floats. This idea is quickly dismissed when it is calculated that the glass floats would cost in excess of $238 million.

- July 17, 1980. Famed explorer Jack Grimm and distinguished oceanographers Dr. William Ryan and Dr. Fred Spiess leave Florida on the research boat *H. J. W. Fay* in an attempt to find the *Titanic*. On July 29, they reach the area in which the *Titanic* sank and begin to crisscross the area, probing the ocean with a sonar device. They leave three weeks later without having found the ship's resting place.

- June 29, 1981. The trio once again set out, this time on the research ship *Gyre*, to the reported *Titanic* site, where they spend nine more days of searching.

Grimm claims a sonar reading indicates a propeller, but nothing definite is found and they once again leave empty handed.

• July 1983. Grimm, Ryan, and Spiess make one final voyage to the *Titanic* site on the *Robert Conrad*. The two weeks of futile search are marred by camera malfunction and high seas. The expedition reports a sonar profile that fits the shape of the *Titanic* but nobody is convinced.

• July 1985. A French research vessel, *Le Suroit*, spends six weeks combing a 150-mile block of sea based on the *Titanic*'s last known position and finds nothing. Among the group of scientists on the *Le Suroit* is geologist Dr. Robert D. Ballard. The main technological advancement in the search is a video system built into a deep ocean minisub called *Argo*.

• August 22, 1985. A follow-up expedition, headed up by Dr. Ballard and including 49 French and American scientists and crew on the research vessel *Knorr*, steams into the same stretch of ocean *Le Suroit* has searched just weeks earlier. Towed behind the *Knorr*, at the 13,000-foot level, is the *Argo*.

• August 22–31. The *Knorr* crisscrosses the ocean with the *Argo* trailing behind. The cameras will spot dunes and the occasional fish but not a hint of wreckage.

• September 1. At 1 A.M., Dr. Ballard is roused from his

sleep. Fellow scientist Jean-Louis Michel has informed him that the Argo has picked up the image of small chunks of metal on the ocean floor.

- 1:05 A.M. A large metal cylinder appears on the screen. It is immediately identified as a boiler. The debris is becoming thicker and a large, shadowy object can be seen approximately 600 yards ahead. Fearing the *Argo* will be damaged, the crew brings it up for the night.

- September 2. Sonar readings indicate it is safe to send the *Argo* back down. Shortly after it reachs bottom, Ballard and the others find that the shadowy object from the previous night is actually a large section of the front part of the *Titanic*. The water was so clear at this level that Ballard and his crew could easily make out anchor chains, beds, unbroken bottles of wine, a silver platter, a chamber pot, and lumps of coal.

- September 2–5. The crew of the *Knorr* continues to discover the wonders of the *Titanic*. The *Argo*'s sister ship *Angus* begins shooting color film of the wreck. At one point the forward part of the *Titanic* suddenly disappears into nothing, and the crew could see that the stern of the ship is missing. On the fifth day of exploring the wreckage, the stern of the *Titanic* is discovered 800 feet away from the rest of the wreck.

- September 5. The *Knorr* leaves the *Titanic* site.

- July 1986. Dr. Ballard returns to the *Titanic* site with a second expedition. This time he brings the robot *Jason Jr.* and the *Alvin, a* small submersible submarine that will allow Ballard and fellow scientists to land on the deck of the *Titanic*. A more detailed exploration takes place, shedding new light on the night the *Titanic* went down.

- The *Alvin's* crew compartment is 7 feet in diameter.

- It takes Ballard's submersibles two and a half hours to reach the ocean floor and two and a half hours to resurface.

- A major event on Ballard's second expedition is the discovery and exploration of the *Titanic's* Grand Staircase area.

- At the end of the second expedition, Ballard leaves a plaque on the ocean floor honoring those who died in the *Titanic* disaster.

- June 30 to July 17, 1991. A Russian-Canadian expedition aboard the research vessel *Akadomik* explores the *Titanic* wreckage.

- A total of 20 men make 17 dives averaging 18 hours each. A total of 139 hours is spent on the ocean floor.

- A total of 40,000 feet of film is shot, which later become the IMAX film *Titanica*.

- The first *Titanic* artifacts are recovered during the

1991 expedition.

• The salvage company RMS *Titanic* Inc., headed by George Tulloch and Arnie Geller, explores the wreckage of the *Titanic* for 15 days in 1993.

• Their submersible is called *Natile*. A total of 15 dives are made in 15 days. Each dive lasts 8 to12 hours. A hundred hours are spent descending and ascending to the *Titanic*.

• An estimated 800 artifacts are recovered. Tulloch will immediately become embroiled in a legal battle over the rights to salvage and sell the *Titanic* items.

• RMS *Titanic* Inc. returns to the site in 1994. Tulloch, in the meantime, has won the right to salvage the *Titanic* on the condition that nothing he find could be sold except for the lumps of coal.

• Each dive during the 1994 expedition costs $100,000 —an estimated $5 per second.

• Tulloch and RMS *Titanic* Inc. return in 1996 for a 30-day stay that runs the entire month of August.

• Their goal is to view the wreck, bring up more items and, with the aid of lift bags and tow lines, bring up a section of the *Titanic*'s hull.

• The section of the hull to be salvaged is from the starboard side of C Deck and includes cabins C 79 and C 81.

• The ship *Ocean Voyager* arrives in mid-August, carrying massive light towers to aid in the salvage operation.

• The salvage operation begins and the hull section rises to within 200 feet of the surface. Unexpectedly Hurricane Edward chooses that moment to enter the North Atlantic and buffet the expedition. The crew wage a gallant battle, but one after another the tow lines snap in the face of the hurricane winds, and the hull falls back to the ocean floor, approximately 10 miles from where it was first discovered.

CHAPTER 13

TITANIC HEADLINES

he newspaper headlines ran quickly and often inaccurately in the hours and days that followed the *Titanic* tragedy. Guided more by emotion and wishful thinking than by fact, early accounts of the sinking of the *Titanic* were often a mixture of half- truths, third- and fourth-hand accounts, and the sketchy bits of fact that were slow to emerge. Consequently two of the first newspaper accounts will go down in history as two of the most inaccurate, as witness the headlines that greeted readers just hours after the disaster.

TITANIC SUNK, NO LIVES LOST
(The London *Daily Mail,* April 16, 1912)

PASSENGERS SAFELY MOVED
AND STEAMER *TITANIC* TAKEN IN TOW
(*The Christian Science Monitor,* April 15, 1912)

Accuracy aside, what was certain was that the world had formed an immediate attachment to the *Titanic* prior to its maiden voyage and that interest con-

112

tinued even in tragedy. A sampling of the headlines that splashed across the world's newspapers continues to be a measure of the bond between everyday people and the elegance that was the *Titanic*.

THE NEW *TITANIC* STRIKES ICEBERG AND CALLS FOR AID, VESSELS RUSH TO HER SIDE
(*The Herald* April 15, 1912)

ALL SAVED FROM *TITANIC* AFTER COLLISION
(*The Evening Sun*, April 15, 1912)

WATCHERS ANGERED BY *CARPATHIA*'S SILENCE (*The Evening Mail*, April 15, 1912)

CARPATHIA LETS NO SECRETS OF THE TITANIC'S LOSS ESCAPE BY WIRELESS
(*The World*, April 15, 1912)

TITANIC REPORTED TO HAVE STRUCK ICEBERG
(The Richmond, Virginia *Times Dispatch*, April 15, 1912)

CRUSHED BY ICEBERG, MIGHTY STEAMER IS ON BRINK OF RUIN
(*The Evening World*, April 15, 1912)

1302 ARE DROWNED OR MISSING
(The Richmond, Virginia *News Leader*, April 16, 1912)

TITANIC DISASTER
(*The London Times*, April 16, 1912)

REPAIR PROBLEM,
NO DOCK LARGE ENOUGH IN AMERICA
(The London *Daily Mail*, April 16, 1912)

UNA GRAN CATASTROFE DE *TITANIC*
(*La Prensa*, Buenos Aires, Argentina, April 16, 1912)

MAJOR BUTT, WITH GUN IN HAND,
HELD BACK FRENZIED MEN, SAVED WOMEN,
CAPTAIN SMITH A SUICIDE ON BRIDGE
(*The Los Angeles Times*, April 16, 1912)

OVER 1500 SINK TO DEATH WITH
GIANT WHITE STAR STEAMER *TITANIC*
(The Landmark, Virginia *Pilot* and
Norfolk *Landmark*, April 16, 1912)

1500 LIVES LOST WHEN *TITANIC* PLUNGES
HEADLONG INTO DEPTHS OF THE SEA
(The *Los Angeles Times*, April 16, 1912)

DEAD 1302, SAVED 868, ENORMITY
OF *TITANIC* SEA TRAGEDY GROWS
(The Richmond, Virginia *Times Dispatch*,
April 17, 1912)

LA CATASTROPHE DU *TITANIC*
(*Le Figaro*, Paris, France, April 17, 1912)

O NAUFRAGIO DO TITANIC
(*O Estado do São Paulo*, São Paulo, Brazil,
April 17, 1912)

KING AND QUEEN HORRIFIED
AT APPALLING DISASTER
(*The Los Angeles Times*, April 19, 1912)

TITANIC'S DEATH LIST, 1601,
ONLY 739 LIVES ARE SAVED
(The Richmond Virginia *Times Dispatch*,
April 19, 1912)

TRAGIC DETAILS OF SINKING OF
TITANIC GIVEN BY WITNESSES
(The Staunton, Virginia *Daily Leader*,
April 19, 1912)

QUEEN OF THE SEAS' AWFUL FATE
ON HER FIRST TRIP OUT
(The Richmond, Virginia *Times Dispatch*,
April 28, 1912)

CHAPTER 14

TITANIC MOVIES

When the *Titanic* went down on April 15, 1912, the public's fascination with the tragedy quickly filtered down through newspapers, magazines, and books to motion picture impresarios. Exhibitors knew there was money to be made on the disaster—and were not going to let the fact that there was very little footage of the actual *Titanic* get in the way of putting warm bodies in movie-house seats.

The first stop for these less-than-scrupulous quick-buck artists was the local film rental outlets, where they snatched up every bit of documentary and stock footage of any and all ocean liners, most conspicuously the *Mauritania* and the *Titanic*'s sister ship *Olympic*. They quickly slapped posters on their marquees, promising the first footage of the *Titanic* disaster.

One glaring example of this *Titanic* ripoff was the owner of a New York movie house who put up a sign that proudly proclaimed *First Pictures of the Titanic* and, in slightly smaller type, the line *Ocean Disaster*. While audiences who were sucked in did get footage

116

of the *Titanic*, it was the often-seen film of the *Titanic* launching.

Theater owners who were a little more honest were able to exploit the interest in the *Titanic* by building film programs around existing *Titanic* footage. The Weber Theater in New York was a prime example. People stood in long lines to see a montage of footage that included the construction of the *Titanic*'s hull in the Belfast, Ireland, shipyards, the ship's launching, images of the rescue ship *Carpathia* and its heroic captain, and some film footage of icebergs floating in the area where the *Titanic* went down. In some houses, theater owners fed the already rabid interest by doctoring documentary footage with images of lifeboats and lifejackets and footage of some of the *Titanic* survivors One of the more enterprising exhibitors would regularly darken the screen and flash the distress signal *CQD* across the footage for added effect.

It was inevitable that documentary footage of the *Titanic* disaster would find its way into the movie houses of the world. But audiences quickly drew tired of cold factual presentations. Theater owners sensed the need for some drama, humanity, and, yes, Hollywood pizazz. In less than a month, the first movie of the *Titanic* disaster was shot and rushed into theaters.

On May 14, 1912, "Saved From the *Titanic*," a 10-minute silent film starring real-life *Titanic* survivor Dorothy Gibson, was wowing audiences. The film, equal parts documentary footage and flimsy romantic plot, did little more than remind audiences of the true magnitude of the *Titanic* disaster.

The next attempt at *Titanic* cinema would not appear until 1943, when a German production company released *Titanic*, a documentary-style propaganda film whose hero, the *Titanic*'s lone German officer, was a totally fictional character.

Television also made occasional stabs at interpreting the *Titanic* mystique. A television version of the *Titanic* incident aired in March 1956. And, years later, the short-lived television series *Time Tunnel*'s debut episode had the intrepid time travelers going back to the deck of the *Titanic* in an attempt to avert the disaster. Needless to say, they failed.

But movies were the place where interest in the *Titanic* continued to grow. More films would follow. And the quality and attention to detail would continue to improve, as well.

Here are some of the more notable attempts to capture the disaster:

SAVED FROM THE TITANIC (1912)

STUDIO: Eclair Moving Picture Company
DIRECTOR: Etienne Arnaud
SCREENWRITER: Etienne Arnaud/Harry Raver
CAST: Dorothy Gibson, Alex Francis, Miss Stuart, Jack Adolfi, William Dunn, Guy Oliver
BUDGET: Unknown

BOX OFFICE: Unknown

STORY: Miss Dorothy is about to embark on the *Titanic* at Cherbourg, France, to return home to marry Ensign Jack. Ensign Jack and Dorothy's parents patiently await a wireless message that will announce the time of her arrival. An impatient Ensign Jack persuades his friends to take him to a nearby wireless post so that he can communicate directly with the *Titanic*. Shortly after they arrive at the wireless post, the distress message from the *Titanic* comes through, telling of the disaster. Ensign Jack and Dorothy's parents spend the next day in anguish as they await word of Dorothy's fate. Dorothy is saved and later tells the story of the wreck of the *Titanic*. Dorothy, thoroughly stressed from the ordeal, faints. Dorothy's mother calls Jack the next day and says that if he wants to marry Dorothy, he must resign from the navy so that his bride to be will never again worry about the perils of the sea. Jack is torn but ultimately decides to stay in the navy. Dorothy's father is so impressed with Jack's decision and dedication to God and country that he calls Dorothy into the room and says, "My daughter, there's your husband."

• The normal time for a one-reel film to be produced, processed and distributed in 1912 was two months. "Saved From the *Titanic*" cut that schedule in half.

• "Saved From the *Titanic*" is reported to have been shot in less than a week.

- Dorothy Gibson wore the same clothes she wore on the *Titanic* in the film.

- The film featured a re-creation of the *Titanic* disaster as Dorothy explained the calamity to her parents and Jack.

- The Eclair Moving Picture Company was a French company with an American branch in Fort Lee, New Jersey.

TITANIC (AKA NEARER MY GOD TO THEE) (1953)

STUDIO: Twentieth Century–Fox

DIRECTOR: Jean Negulesco

WRITER: Charles Brackett, Walter Reisch, Richard Breen.

CAST: Clifton Webb, Barbara Stanwyck, Robert Wagner, Richard Basehart, Audrey Dalton, Thelma Ritter, Brian Aherne.

BUDGET: Not available.

BOX OFFICE: Opened to largely favorable reviews. But even the favorable reviews indicated that the facts were given short shrift in favor of fiction and melodrama.

STORY: The *Titanic* goes totally Hollywood. Fully half the film sets up a number of different story lines surrounding fictional characters and their problems as they come aboard the doomed ocean liner. They include an alcoholic priest, an estranged couple fighting over the custody of their children, and a young man who is falling in love with the couple's daughter. We are fully halfway through the film before the inevitable happens.

Titanic plays fast and loose with the facts, and purists have a field day finding the inconsistencies in the film. But ultimately *Titanic* is well mounted and did result in an Oscar for its screenwriters.

A NIGHT TO REMEMBER (1958)

STUDIO: Rank Films

DIRECTOR: Roy Ward Baker

WRITER: Eric Ambler (based on the Walter Lord book of the same name)

CAST: Kenneth Moore, Jill Dixon, David McCallum, Laurence Naismith, Honor Blackman, Frank Lawton, Alec McCowen, George Rose.

BUDGET: Not available.

BOX OFFICE: *A Night to Remember* opened to rave reviews on December 17, 1958.

STORY: The accurate *Titanic* story done in a near-documentary style details the events leading up to striking the iceberg. Lord's book comes alive in big and small moments.

• Walter Lord researched his book for 20 years.

• The film rights to *A Night to Remember* were acquired on December 2, 1956.

• Ambler's script contained 180 speaking parts.

• The decision was made to film *A Night to Remember* in black and white.

• It was filmed in Pinewood Studios in London and off the coast of Scotland.

• The filmmakers did extensive research on the film, looking at ship's logs and *Titanic*-related paperwork, and interviewing a number of survivors.

• The film used 1,500 extras.

A scale-model *Titanic* was built and sunk. Cost: $25,000.

• The R.M.S. *Asturias* was used as the stand-in for the *Titanic* in the film.

RAISE THE *TITANIC* (1980)

STUDIO: AFD
DIRECTOR: Jerry Jameson
WRITER: Adam Kennedy (Stanley Kramer also worked on early drafts)
CAST: Jason Robards Jr., Richard Jordan, David Selby, Anne Archer, Alec Guinness, J. D. Cannon.
BUDGET: $36 million.
BOX OFFICE: Opened in August, 1980, to horrendous reviews. It managed to bring in $9 million at the box office in the United States before disappearing from theaters. Eventually, it made its cost back, with little profit.
STORY: Seventy years after the *Titanic* sinks, the U.S. government discovers that a powerful new compound called Byzantium was aboard the ship and still exists

in a watertight compartment inside the ship at the bottom of the sea. It turns out that the Russians know about the existence of this element as well. It's a race against time and the Russians in a spy- and double-cross-laden attempt to locate the *Titanic* and bring its valuable cargo to the surface.

• *Raise the Titanic* is based on the novel by Clive Cussler.

• Cussler sold the paperback rights to *Raise the Titanic* for $800,000. He sold the film rights for $450,000.

• Stanley Kramer was hired to direct.

• The production allowed 24 weeks for filming.

• *Raise the Titanic* was filmed on location in Los Angeles, San Diego, Greece, Alaska, and Malta.

• A tank for the sequences in which the *Titanic* is raised was built in Malta. Its dimensions were 300 feet across at the top and 150 feet wide at the bottom. When filled, it held 9 million gallons of water.

• A mockup of the *Titanic* was built at a cost of $3 million. It was 55 feet long and 12 feet high and weighed 10,000 pounds.

• At one point in preproduction, the *Queen Mary* was being considered as a stand-in for the *Titanic* when it is raised to the surface. The $2 million price tag to rent the ship proved a deal breaker.

- A replacement was found in Greece in the derelict ship, *Athinai*.

- Stanley Kramer quit two weeks into filming, citing creative differences with the producers. He was replaced by Jerry Jameson, whose previous watery credit was *Airport '77*.

- The U.S. Navy initially balked at providing support to the film because they did not like the way U.S. military types and Russians were portrayed in the script. Some changes were made and the navy came through with ships, men, and aircraft for various scenes in the film.

- The famous Mayflower Hotel makes an appearance in one scene in the film.

- A number of scenes were filmed in the natural caves in the Hollywood Hills. Because the scenes required that these be ice caves, the production spent $80,000 to coat the tunnels with white plastic to simulate ice.

- Clive Cussler did a cameo in a scene with Robards and Selby.

- The production's budget included $22,000 a day for diesel fuel.

- Divers pulled ropes attached to the *Titanic* mockup to give it the illusion of movement.

TITANIC (1997)

STUDIO: Paramount-Twentieth Century Fox
DIRECTOR: James Cameron
WRITER: James Cameron
CAST: Leonardo DiCaprio, Kate Winslet, Billy Zane, Kathy Bates, Frances Fisher, Bernard Hill, Jonathan Hyde, Danny Nucci, David Warner, Bill Paxton.
BUDGET: $200 million plus.
BOX OFFICE: The film opened in December 1997. At publication time, it has remained the number one film for thirteen straight weeks and made nearly $500 million, and has been nominated for 14 Academy Awards.
STORY: The story of the *Titanic* begins in the present, two and a half miles down at the site of the famous ship's watery grave, where treasure hunter Brock Lovett discovers an artifact that leads to Rose Calvert, a survivor of that tragic night, and to a first-hand account of the events that led to the sinking. Rose's memories return to the day when the *Titanic*, in a gala spectacle typical of those opulent times, is being loaded with passengers for its maiden voyage. Amid the splendor, Rose DeWitt Bukater, a 17-year-old member of the upper crust, makes the acquaintance of a free-spirited young artist named Jack Dawson. Their infatuation is immediate and, as the *Titanic* makes its way into the open waters of the North Atlantic, it blossoms into love. It appears that nothing can stand in the way of romance ... not even an iceberg.

THE MAKING OF *TITANIC*

- *Titanic*, in the earliest stages of preproduction, went under the working title *Planet Ice*.

- James Cameron's previous ocean-going movies were *The Abyss* and *Piranha II: The Spawning*.

- James Cameron's inspiration for *Titanic* came from the expeditions of Dr. Robert Ballard. For Cameron, Ballard's discoveries answered many questions about the *Titanic*'s demise but also asked some questions he felt needed answering.

- "The tragedy of the *Titanic* has assumed an almost mythic quality in our collective imaginations," said Cameron. "But the passage of time had robbed it of its human face and vitality. I hoped that this movie would allow viewers to once again invest their hearts and minds."

- Early in 1995, Cameron met with *Titanic* experts Don Lynch and Ken Marschall. He requested that they go through his *Titanic* treatment page by page, and point out any physical and historical innacuracies.

- "Jim wanted to know, for instance, if a character could be on the racquetball court one minute and by the swimming pool the next without going up three decks, walking the length of the ship, and going down five decks," said Lynch. "He wanted all the action to be possible, even if only the real diehard *Titanic* enthusiasts would know."

• Lynch and Marschall supplied Cameron with samples and photographs of furnishings, carvings, and fabrics from their personal collection of artifacts from *Titanic*'s sister ship *Olympic*.

• Cameron's early research turned up these facts about the survival chances on the *Titanic*: A male in third class had a 1 in 10 chance of survival. A male in first class had a 50/50 chance of survival. A first-class female had nearly a 100 percent chance of survival. A third-class female had a 25 percent chance of survival.

• Cameron, always a thorough researcher, stated that he could not go ahead with the production of *Titanic* unless he could actually film the remains of the *Titanic* himself.

• In 1995 Cameron chartered the Russian research vessel *Keldysh,* which contained the two submersible mini subs *Mir 1* and *Mir 2.* Each sub had room for three people in its seven-foot diameter crew area.

• Cameron proposed a series of 12 dives to the *Titanic* site to film the footage that would appear at the beginning of his film.

• Each dive would take 16 hours. Five of those 16 hours

consisted of ascending and descending to the *Titanic* wreck site.

- The camera held a 500-foot load of film. It was the equivalent of 12 minutes of actual shooting time.

- The water pressure on the underwater cameras was 6,000 pounds per square inch.

- During one of the dives, the batteries in Cameron's submersible died. The weather topside was bad, so Cameron sat on the ocean floor for hours waiting for another sub to come and rescue them.

- Cameron later remembered that, while he was on the bottom, "I was just sitting there, thinking Christ! This is it! I'm going to die!"

- The rescue sub finally arrived with a new battery. Cameron continued to make the dives. Cameron stayed at the *Titanic* site for a total of three months.

- The Wellan Davit Company, which made the davits for the real *Titanic*, built the film *Titanic*'s davits to their original plans.

- The *Titanic*'s original shipbuilders, Harland and Wolff gave the filmmakers copies of the ship's original blueprints and Thomas Andrew's early notebook. This was the first time this material had ever been made available outside the shipbuilding complex.

- BMK Stoddard, the company who manufactured the

carpeting in the dining saloon and reception room of *Titanic*'s D deck, offered the pattern of the dye of the carpeting.

- *Titanic*'s art department also faithfully reproduced deck chairs, table lamps, leaded windows, crystal, china, luggage, and lifejackets.

- More than 450 wigs and several hundred hairpieces were made for the cast and extras in the film.

- The *Titanic* production crew originally scouted locations in Malta, Poland, the United Kingdom, Australia, the United States, and Canada but found that none of the proposed locations could handle the immense scale of the climactic scenes in the film.

- During this period, Cameron and the production company held a series of meetings designed to come up with the final design of the *Titanic*. A model was made and videotaped.

- The *Titanic* sessions resulted in plans for a nearly full-sized exterior ship set that would be 775 feet long and would stand 45 feet from the water line to the boat deck floor. Interior sets, including the first-class dining saloon and the three-story Grand Staircase, would be built nearly full scale. The interior staterooms and such sets as the reception room, smoking room, gymnasium and Palm Court Café were reproduced with the aid of old *Titanic* and *Olympic* photos.

- The ship was hinged at various points for the sinking sequences.

- A decision was made in May 1996 to custom build a studio on the shores of Rosarito Beach, Mexico.

- Construction began on May 30, 1996. A hundred days later the newly christened Fox Baja Studios was open for business.

- The Fox Baja Studio contained a 17-million-gallon exterior tank in which the *Titanic* was sunk, a 5-million-gallon interior tank housed in a 32,000-square-foot soundstage, three traditional stages, and production and wardrobe facilities.

- Kate Winslet prepared for her role by taking etiquette lessons. She also had to learn to speak with an upper-class Philadelphia accent.

- Leonardo DiCaprio created his own dance steps for the dance sequence in the film. He had to learn how to handle a fork in the upper crust style.

- When no artist could be found for the sequence in which Jack was to sketch Rose, Cameron stepped in and did the drawing.

- *Titanic* is Bill Paxton's fourth movie with James Cameron.

- Cameron based the character of Rose Calvert on the real-life artist Beatrice Wood.

- Filming on *Titanic* offically began in July 1996 in a shooting tank located in Escondido, California, where a re-creation of the *Titanic*'s exteriors and interiors was filmed for the opening sequences.

- Cameron moved to Halifax, Nova Scotia, to film the wraparound sequences to *Titanic*. Appearing in the sequences are the Russian research vessel *Keldysh* and Dr. Anatoly M. Sagalevitch, the director of the scientific institute that operates the *Keldysh*.

- More than 1,000 extras were used in *Titanic*. Some spoke English. Some spoke Spanish. Crew people who could speak both were at a premium.

- James Cameron was fond of throwing cellular phones during filming. He once got so angry that he threw a phone all the way over the ship and into the ocean.

- Scenes in *Titanic* averaged 30 to 40 takes each.

- Actor Mark Lindsay Chapman, who portrayed Chief Officer Wilde, was fired off the picture twice. He was immediately hired back each time. "He only fires people he likes," chuckled Chapman, "so I consider the firings an honor."

- The *Titanic* exterior set hinges were supposed to fold during the scene in which the *Titanic* sinks. During one take, however, the hinges broke, and rather than sending the ship down 12 feet, it went down 47 feet and broke through both of the ship's control decks.

- Mark Lindsay Chapman nearly became the *Titanic*'s one true fatality during the filming of one element of the sinking. He was hit in the back by a lifeboat and fell unconscious into the ocean. The next thing Chapman remembers is "waking up, it was daylight and I was on a resuscitator." Cameron, it should be noted, kept filming throughout Chapman's ordeal.

- 100 stuntmen were used in the tilting poop deck sequence.

- During one of the climactic sequences, more than 5 million gallons of filtered sea water were funneled into the tank on Stage 2.

CHAPTER 15

KEEPING THE
MEMORY ALIVE

The *Titanic* Historical Society met for the first time in 1963. But the seeds of the organization dedicated to keeping the memory of the *Titanic* alive had already been planted years earlier.

"I'd have to say that my fascination with the *Titanic* began in 1953," recalled *Titanic* Historical Society president and founder Edward Kamuda. "I had seen the *Titanic* movie with Clifton Webb and had, just prior to that, read a short story about the *Titanic* called 'A Great Ship Goes Down.' I was just hooked."

The *Titanic* Historical Society was, from the beginning, an informal mixture of enthusiasts and actual *Titanic* survivors. Twenty-five *Titanic* survivors were members during the early years, with the number increasing to 50 at its zenith. Currently six surviving *Titanic* passengers are counted among the more than 6,000 members worldwide.

The *Titanic* Historical Society, whose headquarters and museum are based in Springfield, Massachusetts, are keeping the memory of the *Titanic* alive on a number of fronts. The museum, which contains prediscovery artifacts as well as photos and documents related to the *Titanic* and the White Star Line, offers visitors a look back into the life and times surrounding the *Titanic*'s maiden voyage. Among the items on display are the model of the ship used in the 1953 movie *Titanic* and the actual lifejacket worn by Madeleine Astor. The society also puts out a quarterly magazine, called *Titanic Commutator* which carries survivor accounts of the voyage, the latest news on the *Titanic* in the media, and announcements of coming books and videos on the subject.

The society also sponsors yearly tours of *Titanic* - related towns and cities. In the past the *Titanic* Historical Society has visited Belfast; Queenstown, Ireland; and Southampton, England. Yearly *Titanic* conventions are held on the April 15 anniversary of the sinking. The 1998 convention will be held in Springfield, Massachussets.

Kamuda is amused by the increased interest in the *Titanic* with the release of the big-budget motion picture. "Everybody is trying to jump into the pool right now because the *Titanic* is a hot item. But for us, it has always been."

For membership and other information on the *Titanic* Historical Society and its activities write: *Titanic* Historical Society, P.O. Box 51053, Indian Orchard, MA 01151-0053.

CHAPTER 16

THE PASSENGER LIST

The publishing of steamship passenger lists was a common item in major newspapers in 1912. Following the *Titanic* disaster, newspapers all over the world rushed out this list of all passengers known to be aboard the *Titanic*.

And typical of the passenger lists of the day, it is not the perfect beast. Some passengers only gave last names or initials. Married couples often went by Mr. and Mrs. and the husband's first names. Some passengers did not give their real names. Why? For the professional gamblers on board, the reason was obvious. For the unmarried couples traveling together—and the report is that there were a handful of those on the *Titanic*—the attitude and the times dictated they travel as Mr. and Mrs.

What follows is a list of *Titanic* passengers and when they embarked on the ocean liner. The survivors' names are in boldface.

FIRST-CLASS PASSENGERS

Miss Elizabeth Walton Allen, Mr. H. J. Allison, Mrs. H. J. Allison and **Maid**, Miss L. Allison, **Master T.**

Allison and Nurse, Mr. Harry Anderson, Miss Cornelia I. Andrews, Mr. Thomas Andrews, **Mrs. E. D. Appleton**, Mr. Ramon Artagaveytia, Colonel J. J. Astor and Manservant, **Mrs. J. J. Astor and Maid, Mrs. N. Aubert and Maid**.

Mr. A. H. Barkworth, Mr. J. Baumann, **Mrs. James Baxter**, Mr. Quigg Baxter, Mr. T. Beattie, **Mr. R. L. Beckwith, Mrs. R. L. Beckwith, Mr. K. H. Behr**. **Mr. D. H. Bishop, Mrs. D. H. Bishop**, Mr. H. Bjornstrom, Mr. Stephen Weart Blackwell, **Mr. Henry Blank, Miss Caroline Bonnell, Miss Lily Bonnell**, Mr. J. J. Borebank, **Miss Bowen, Miss Elsie Bowerman**, Mr. John B. Brady, Mr. E. Brandeis, **Mr. George Brayton**, Dr. Arthur Jackson Brewe, **Mrs. J. J. Brown, Mrs. J. M. Brown, Mrs. W. Bucknell and Maid**, Major Archibald W. Butt.

Mr. E. P. Calderhead, Mrs. Churchill Candee,. Mrs. J.W.M. Cardoza and Maid, **Mr. T.D.M. Cardoza** and Manservant, Mr. Frank Carlson, Mr. F. M. Carran, Mr. J. P. Carran, **Mr. William E. Carter, Mrs. William E. Carter** and Maid, **Miss Lucile Carter, Master William T. Carter** and Manservant, Mr. Howard B. Case, **Mrs. H. A. Cassebeer**, Mr. T. W. Cavendish, **Mrs. T. W. Cavendish and Maid**, Mr. Herbert F. Chaffee, **Mrs. Herbert F. Chaffee, Mr. N. C. Chambers, Mrs. N. C. Chambers, Miss Gladys Cherry, Mr. Paul Chevre, Mrs. E. M. Bowerman Chibnafl**

Mr. Robert Chisholm, Mr. Walter M. Clark, **Mrs. Walter M. Clark**, Mr. George Quincy Clifford, Mr. E. P. Colley, **Mrs. A. T. Compton, Miss S. P. Compton**, Mr. A. T. Compton Jr., **Mrs. R. G. Cornell**, Mr. John B. Crafton, Mr. Edward G. Crosby, **Mrs. Edward G. Crosby, Miss Harriet Crosby**, Mr. John Bradley Cummings, **Mrs. John Bradley Cummings**.

Mr. P. D. Daly, Mr. Robert W. Daniel, Mr. Thornton Davidson, **Mrs. Thornton Davidson, Mrs. B. de Villiers, Mr. A. A. Dick, Mrs. A. A. Dick, Dr. Washington Dodge, Mrs. Washington Dodge, Master Washington Dodge, Mrs. F. C. Douglas**, Mr. W. D. Douglas, **Mrs. W. D. Douglas** and Maid, Mr. William C. Dulles.

Mrs. Boulton Earnshew, Miss Caroline Endres, Miss E. M. Eustis, Miss. E. Evans.

Mrs. A. Flegenheim, Mr. J. I. Flynn, Mr. B. L. Foreman, Mr. Mark Fortune, Mrs. Mark Fortune, **Miss Ethel Fortune, Miss Alice Fortune**. **Miss Mabel Fortune**, Mr. Charles Fortune, Mr. T. P. Franklin, **Mr. T. G. Frauenthal, Dr. Henry W. Frauenthal, Mrs. Henry W. Frauenthal, Miss Marguerite Frolicher**, Mr. J. Futrelle, **Mrs. J. Futrelle**.

Mr. Arthur Gee, **Mrs. L. Gibson, Miss D. Gibson**, Mr. Victor Giglio, **Mr. S. L. Goldenberg, Mrs. S. L. Goldenberg**, Mrs. George B. Goldschmidt, **Sir Cosmo Duff Gordon, Lady Duff Gordon and Maid, Colonel Archibald Gracie**, Mr. Graham, **Mrs. William G.**

Graham, Miss Margaret Graham, Mrs. L. D. Greenfield, Mrs. W. B. Greenfield, Mr. Benjamin Guggenheim.

Mr. George A. Harder, Mrs. George A. Harder, Mr. Henry Sleeper Harper and Manservant, Mrs. Henry Sleeper Harper, Mr. Henry B. Harris, **Mrs. Henry B. Harris,** Mr. W. H. Harrison, **Mr. H. Haven, Mr. W. J. Hawksford,** Mr. Charles M. Hays, **Mrs. Charles M. Hays** and Maid, **Miss Margaret Head Hays, Mr. Christopher Hays,** Mr. Herbert Henry Hilliard, Mr. W. E. Hipkins, **Mrs. Ida S. Hippach, Miss Jean Hippach, Mrs. John C. Hogeboom,** Mr. A. O. Holverson, **Mrs. A. O. Holverson, Mr. Frederick M. Hoyt, Mrs. Frederick M. Hoyt,** Mr. W. F. Holt.

Mrs. A. E. Isham, **Mr. J. Bruce Ismay** and Manservant.

Mr. Birnbaum Jakob, Mr. C. C. Jones, Mr. H. F. Julian.

Mr. Edward A. Kent, Mr. F. R. Kenyon, **Mrs. F. R. Kenyon, Mr. E. N. Kimball, Mrs. E. N. Kimball,** Mr. Herman Klaber.

Mr. Fletcher Fellows Williams-Lambert, **Mrs. F. A. Leader.** Mr. E. G. Lewy, **Mrs. J. Lindstroem, Mrs. Ernest H. Lines, Miss Mary C. Lines,** Mr. Edward Lingrey, Mr. Milton C. Long, **Miss Gretchen F. Langley,** Mr. J. H. Loring.

Miss Georgette Alexandra Madill, Mr. J. E. Maguire, **Mr. Pierre Marechal,** Mr. D. W. Marvin, **Mrs. D. W.**

Marvin, Mr. T. McCaffry, Mr. Timothy J. McCarthy, **Mr. J. R. McGough**, Mr. Edgar J. Meyer, **Mrs. Edgar J. Meyer**, Mr. Frank D. Millet, Dr. W. E. Missahan, **Mrs. W.B. Missahan, Miss Daisy Missahan, Mr. Pkdtp E. Moch**, Mr. Phillip E. Moch, Mr. H. Markland Molson, Mr. Clarence Moore and Manservant.

Mr. Charles Natsch, Mr. A. W. Newell, **Miss Alice Newell, Miss Madeline Newell, Miss Helen Newsom**, Mr. A. S. Nicholson.

Mr. F. Omont, Mr. E. C. Ostby, **Miss Helen R. Ostby**, Mr. S. Ovies.

Mr. M.H.W. Parr, Mr. Austin Partner, Mr. V. Payne, Mr. Thomas Pears, **Mrs. Thomas Pears**, Mr. Victor Penasco, **Mrs. Victor Penasco** and Maid, **Major Arthur Peuchen**, Mr. Walter Chamberlain Porter, **Mrs. Thomas Potter Jr.**

Mr. Jonkheer J. G. Reuchlin, **Mr. George Rheims, Mrs. Edward S. Robert and Maid**, Mr. Washington A. Roebling 2nd, **Mr. C. Rolmane**, Mr. Hugh R. Rood, **Miss Rosenbaum**, Mr. J. Hugo Ross, **The Countess of Rothes and Maid**, Mr. M. Rothschild, **Mrs. M. Rothschild**, Mr. Alfred Rowe, Mr. Arthur Ryerson, **Mrs. Arthur Ryerson and Maid, Miss Emily Ryerson, Miss Susan Ryerson, Master Jack Ryerson**.

Mr. Adolphe Saalfeld, Mrs. Paul Schabert, Mr. Frederick K. Seward, Miss E. W. Shutes, Mr. S. V. Silver-

thorne, Mr. William B. Silvey, **Mrs. William B. Silvey, Mr. Oberst Altons Simonius, Mr. William T. Sloper,** Mr. John M. Smart, Mr. J. Clinch Smith, Mr. R. W. Smith, Mr. L. P. Smith, **Mrs. L. P. Smith, Mr. John Snyder, Mrs. John Snyder, Mr. A. L. Soloman, Mr. Frederick O. Spedden, Mrs. Frederick O. Spedden and Maid, Master R. Douglas Spedden and Nurse,** Mr. W. A. Spencer, **Mrs. W. A. Spencer** and Maid, **Dr. Max Stahelin,** Mr. W. T. Stead, **B. B. Steffanson, H. B. Steffanson, Mr. Max Frolicher Stehli, Mrs. Max Frolicher Stehli, Mr. C.E.H. Stengel, Mrs. C.E.H. Stengel,** Mr. A. A. Stewart, **Mrs. George M. Stone and Maid,** Mr. Isidor Straus and Manservant, Mrs. Isidor Straus and Maid, Mr. Frederick Sutton, **Mrs. Frederick Joel Swift.**

Mr. Emil Taussig, **Mrs. Emil Taussig, Miss Ruth Taussig, Mr. E. Z. Taylor, Mrs. E. Z. Taylor,** Mr. J. B. Thayer, **Mrs. J. B. Thayer and Maid, Mr. J. B. Thayer Jr.,** Mr. G. Thorne, **Mrs. G. Thorne, Mr. G. M. Tucker Jr.**

Mr. M. R. Uruchurtu.

Mr. Wyckoff Van der Hoef.

Mr. W. Anderson Walker, Mr. F. M. Warren, **Mrs. F. M. Warren, Mr. J. Weir,** Mr. Percival W. White, Mr. Richard F. White, **Mrs. J. Stuart White and Maid and Manservant,** Mr. George D. Wick, **Mrs. George D. Wick, Miss Mary Wick,** Mr. George D. Widener and

Manservant, **Mrs. George D. Widener and Maid**, Mr. Harry Widener, **Miss Constance Willard**, Mr. Duane Williams, **Mr. R. N. Williams Jr., Mr. Hugh Woolner**, Mr. George Wright.

Miss Marie Young.

SECOND-CLASS PASSENGERS

Mr. Samson Abelson, **Mrs. Hanna Abelson**, Mr. C. Aldworth, Mr. Edgar Andrew, Mr. Frank Andrew, Mr. William Angle, **Mrs. Angle**, Mr. John Ashby.

Mr. Percy Baily, Mr. Chas. R. Baimbridge, **Mrs. Ada E. Balls**, Mr. Frederick J. Banfield, Mr. Robert J. Bateman, **Mr. Edward Beane, Mrs. Ethel Beane**, Mr. H. J. Beauchamp, **Mrs. A. O. Becker and three children, Mr. Lawrence Beesley, Miss Lilian W. Bentham**, Mr. William Berriman, Mr. W. Hull Botsford, Mr. Solomon Bowenur, Mr. Jas. H. Bracken, Mr. Jose de Brito, **Miss Mildred Brown**, Mr. S. Brown, Mrs. Brown, **Miss E. Brown**, Mr. Curt Bryhl, **Miss Dagmar Bryhl, Miss Kate Buss**, Mr. Reginald Butler, Rev. Thomas R. D. Byles, **Miss Karolina Bystrom**.

Mr. Albert F. Caldwell, Mrs. Sylvia Caldwell, Master Alden G. Caldwell, Miss Clear Cameron, Mr. William Carbines, Rev. Ernest C. Carter,. Mrs. Lillian Carter, Mr. John H. Chapman, Mrs. Elizabeth Chapman, Mr. Charles Chapman, **Mrs. Alice Christy, Miss Juli Christy**, Mr. Charles V. Clarke, **Mrs. Ada Maria**

Clarke, Mr. R. C. Coleridge, Mr. Erik Collander, **Mr. Stuart Collett**, Mr. Harvey Collyer, **Mrs. Charlotte Collyer, Miss Marjorie Collyer**, Mrs. Irene Corbett, Mrs. C. P. Corey, Mr. Harry Cotterill.

Mr. Charles Davies, **Mrs. Agnes Davis, Master John M. Davis, Miss Mary Davis**, Mr. Percy Deacon, Mr. Sebastian del Carlo, Mrs. del Carlo, Mr. Herbert Denbou, Mr. William Dibden, **Mrs. Ada Doling, Miss Elsie Doling**, Mr. William J. Downton, **Baron von Drachstedt**, Mr. James V. Drew, **Mrs. Lulu Drew, Master Marshall Drew, Miss Florentina Duran, Miss Asimcion Duran**.

Mr. G. F. Eitemiller, Mr. Ingvar Enander, Mr. Arnie J. Fahlstrom, Mr. Harry Faunthorpe, **Mrs. Lizzie Faunthrope**, Mr. Charles Fillbrook, Mr. Stanley H. Fox, Miss Annie Funk, Mr. Jos. Fynney.

Mr. Harry Gale, Mr. Shadrach Gale, **Miss Ethel Garside**, Mr. Alfred Gaskell, Mr. Lawrence Gavey, Mr. William Gilbert, Mr. Edgar Giles, Mr. Fred Giles, Mr. Ralph Giles, Mr. John Gill, Mr. William Gillespie, Mr. Hans K. Givard, Mr. Samuel Greenberg.

Mr. Reginald Hale, **Mrs. Anna Hamalainer and Infant**, Mr. Wm. H. Harbeck, Mr. John Harper, **Miss Nina Harper, Mr. George Harris**, Mr. Walter Harris, Mr. Benjamin Hart, **Mrs. Esther Hart, Miss Eva Hart, Miss Alice Herman, Mrs. Jane Herman, Miss Kate Herman**, Mr. Samuel Herman, **Mrs. Mary D.**

Hewlett, Mr. Leonard Hickman, Mr. Lewis Hickman, Mr. Stanley Hickman, Miss Martha Hiltunen, Mr. George Hocking, **Mrs. Elizabeth Hocking, Miss Nellie Hocking**, Mr. Samuel J. Hocking, Mr. Henry P. Hodges, Mr. Hoffman and **two children (Loto and Louis), Mrs. Annie Hold**, Mr. Stephen Hold, Mr. Ambrose Hood, **Mr. Masabumi Hosono**, Mr. Benjamin Howard, Mrs. Ellen T. Howard, Mr. George Hunt.

Miss Bertha Ilett.

Mrs. Amy P. Jacobsohn, Mr. Sidney S. Jacobsohn, Mr. John D. Jarvis, Mr. Clifford Jefferys, Mr. Ernest Jeffreys, Mr. Stephen Jenkin, **Mrs. A. T. Jervan**.

Mrs. Miriam Kantor, Mr. Sehua Kantor, Mrs. J. F. Karnes. Mr. Daniel Keane, **Miss Nora A. Keane, Mrs. F. Kelly**, Rev. Charles L. Kirkland, Mr. John Henrik Kvillner.

Mrs. Anna Lahtinen, Mr. William Lahtinen, Mr. J. J. Lamb, **Mrs. Ameliar Lamore**, Mr. Joseph Laroche, **Mrs. Juliet Laroche, Miss Louise Laroche, Miss Simonne Laroche, Miss Bertha Lehman, Miss Jessie Leitch**, Mr. R. J. Levy, Mr. Robert W. N. Leyson, Mr. John Lingan, Mr. Charles Louch, **Mrs. Alice Adela Louch**.

Mrs. Mary Mack, Mr. Noel Malachard, Mr. A. Mallet, **Mrs. Mallett, Master A. Mallett**, Mr. Emilio Mangiavacchi, Mr. Joseph Mantvila, Mr. Marshall,

Mrs. Kate Marshall, Mr. W. J. Matthews, Mr. Frank H. Maybery, Mr. Arthur G. McCrae, Mr. James McCrie, Mr. Peter D. McKane, **Mr. William Mellers, Mrs. Elizabeth Mellinger and child,** Mr. August Meyer, Mr. Jacob C. Milling, Mr. Henry Mitchell, Dr. Ernest Morawick, Mr. Thomas C. Mudd, Mr. Thomas F. Myles.

Mr. Nicolas Nasser, **Mrs. Nasser,** Mr. Israel Nesson, Mr. Joseph C. Nicholls, Mr. Robert D. Norman, **Mrs. Elizabeth Nye.**

Mr. Richard Otter, **Mr. P. Thomas Oxenham.**

Mr. Julian Padro, Dr. Alfred Pain, **Mr. Emilio Pallas,** Mr. Clifford R. Parker, **Mrs. L. Davis Parrish,** Mr. Frederick Pengelly, Mr. Rene Pernot, Rev. Jos. M. Peruschitz, Mr. Robert Phillips, **Miss Alice Phillips, Miss Rosa Pinsky,** Mr. Martin Ponesell, **Mr. Emilio Portaluppi,** Mr. Frank Pulbaun.

Mrs. Jane Quick, Miss Vera W. Quick, Miss Phyllis Quick.

Mr. David Reeves, Mr. Peter H. Renouf, **Miss Lillie Renouf, Miss E. Reynolds,** Mr. Emile Richard, **Mrs. Emily Richards, Master William Richards, Master George Richards, Miss Lucy Ridsdale,** Mr. Harry Rogers, **Miss Selina Rogers, Miss Emily Rugg.**

Mr. C.F.W. Sedgwick, Mr. Percival Sharp, **Mrs. Imanita Shelley, Miss Lyyli Silven, Miss Maude**

Sincook, Miss Anna Sinkkenen, Mr. Ernest A. Sjostedt, **Miss H. M. Slayter**, Mr. Richard J. Slemen, Mr. Augustus Smith, **Miss Marion Smith**, Mr. Hayden Sobey, Mr. S. Ward Stanton, Mr. Phillip J. Stokes, Mr. George Swane, Mr. George Sweet.

Miss Ellen Toomey, Miss Jessie Trant, Mr. Moses A. Tronpiansky, **Miss E. Celia Troutt**, Dorothy M. Tupin, Mr. William J. Turpin.

Mr. James Veale.

Miss Nellie Walcroft, Mrs. Florence L. Ware, Mr. John James Ware, Mr. William J. Ware, **Miss Bertha Watt, Mrs. Bessie Watt, Miss Susie Webber**, Mr. Leopold Weisz, **Mrs. Matilda Weisz, Mrs. Addie Wells, Miss J. Wells, Master Ralph Wells**, Mr. E. Arthur West, **Mrs. Ada West, Miss Barbara West, Miss Constance West**, Mr. Edward Wheadon, Mr. Edwin Wheeler.

THIRD-CLASS PASSENGERS

BRITISH SUBJECTS EMBARKED AT SOUTHAMPTON

Eugene Abbott, **Rosa Abbott**, Rossmore Abbott, Anthony Abbing, J. Adams, **Filly Aks, Leah Aks**, William Alexander, William Allen, Owen G. Allum, **Emily Badman**, David Barton, W. T. Beavan, A. van Billiard, James Billiard (child), Walter Billiard (child), **Lee Bing**, David Bowen, Lewis Braund, Owen Braund, William Brocklebank.

Erenst Cann, A. Carver, Francesco Celotti, **Chang Chip**, Emil Christmann, **Gurshon Cohen**, Jacob Cook, Harry Corn, **Winnie Coutts, William Coutts (child), Leslie Coutts (child)**, Daniel Coxon, Ernest James Crease, John Hatfield Cribb, **Alice Cribb, Charles Dahl**, Evan Davies, Alfred Davies, John Davies, Joseph Davies, Thomas H. Davison, **Mary Davison**, Mr. Bertram F. Dean, **Mrs. Hetty Dean, Bertran Dean (child), Vera Dean (infant)**, Samuel Dennis, William Dennis, **Edward Derkings, Elizabeth Dowdell, Jenie Drapkin, Joseph Dugemin**.

James Elsbury, **Ethet Emanuel (child)**, Thomas J. Everett, **Choong Foo**, Arthur Ford, Margaret Ford, Mrs. D. M. Ford, Mr. E. W. Ford, M.W.T.N. Ford, Maggie Ford (child), Charles Franklin.

John Garthfirth, Leslie Gilinski, **Frederick Godwin**, Frank J. Goldsmith, **Emily A. Goldsmith, Frank J. W. Goldsmith**, Augusta Goldsmith, Lillian A. Goodwin, Charles E. Goodwin, William F. Goodwin (child), Jessie Goodwin (child), Harold Goodwin (child), Sidney Goodwin (child), George Green, Robert Guest, Alice Harknett, Abraham Harmer, **Ling Hee, May Howard, Abraham Hyman**.

Mr. A. Johnson, Mr. W. Johnson, A. G. Johnston, Mrs. Johnston, William Johnston (child), Mrs. C. H. Johnston, Arthur Keefe, James Kelly, **Ali Lam**, Len Lam, **Fang Lang**, Mr. L. Leonard, J. Lester, Lee Ling,

Simon Lithman, Cordelia Lobb, William A. Lobb, Edward Lockyer, John Lovell.

George W. MacKay, Simon Maisner, Eileen McNamee, Neal McNamee, Marian O. Meanwell, Annie L. Meek, Alfonso Meo, Frank Miles, **Beile Moor**, **Meier Moor**, Leonard C. Moore, William Morley, Rahamin Moutal, Joseph Murdlin, W. H. Nancarrow, Sander Niklasen, Richard C. Nosworthy, Alfred Peacock, Treasteall Peacock, Treasteall Peacock (child), Ernest Pearce, Joseph Peduzzi, John Henry Perkin, Marius Peterson, George Potchett.

Sarah Rath, James George Reed, Harold Reynolds, Emma Risien, Samuel Risien, Alexander Robins, Charity Robins, William John Rogers, Richard H. Rouse, Alfred George J. Rush, Harry Sadowitz, John Sage, Annie Sage, Stella Sage, George Sage, Douglas Sage, Frederick Sage, Dorothy Sage, William Sage (child), Ada Sage (child), Constance Sage (child), Thomas Sage (child), Sinon Sather, W. H. Saundercock, Frederick Sawyer, Maurice Scrota, Frederick Shellard, Charles Shorney, John Simmons, Selman Slocovski, Francis W. Somerton, Woolf Spector, Henry Spinner, **Amy Stanley**, Mr. E. R. Stanley, Mr. T. Storey, **Victor Sunderland**, Henry Sutehall.

Thomas Theobald, Alex Thomas, **Florence Thorney-croft**, Ernest P. Tomlin, Ernest Torber, **Berk Trem-bisky**, **W. Tunquist**, Frederick Ware, Charles W.

Warren, James Webber, **Ellen Wilkes**, Edward Willey, Harry Williams, Leslie Williams, Einar Windelov, Philip Wiseman.

FOREIGNERS EMBARKED AT SOUTHAMPTON

Karen Abelseth, **Olaus Abelseth**, **August Abramson**, Mauritz Adahl, **Humblin Adolf**, Johanna Ahlin, Ali Ahmed, Ilmari Alhomaki, William Ali, Alfreda Anderson, **Erna Anderson**, Albert Anderson, Anders Anderson, Samuel Anderson, Sigrid Anderson (child), Thor Anderson, **Carla Anderson**, Ingeborg Anderson (child), Ebba Anderson (child), Sigvard Anderson (child), Ellis Anderson, Ida Augusta Anderson, Paul Edvin Anderson, Minko Angheloff, Carl Asplund (child), Charles Asplund, **Felix Asplund (child)**, Gustaf Asplund (child), **Johan Asplund**, **Lillian Asplund (child)**, Oscar Asplund (child), **Selma Asplund**, Joseph Arnold, Josephine Arnold, Ernest Axel A. Aronsson, Adola Asim, Ali Assam, Albert Augustsan.

Karl Backstrom, **Marie Backstrom**, Cerin Balkic, John Viktor Benson, Ivar Berglund, Hans Berkeland, Ernst Bjorklund, Guentcho Bostandyeff, Elin Ester Braf, Carl R. Brobek, Grego Cacic, Luka Cacic, Maria Cacic, Manda Cacic, Peter Calie, Carl R. Carlson, Julius Carlsson, August Sigfrid Carlsson, Domingos Fernardeo Coelho, Fotio Coleff, Peyo Coleff, Bartol Cor, Ivan Cor, Ludovik Cor, **Mauritz Dahl**, Gerda Dahlberg, Branko Dakic, Ernest Danbom, Gillber

Danbom (infant), Sigrid Danoff, Yoto Danoff, Khristo Dantchoff, Regyo Delalic, Mito Denkoff, Jovan Dimic, Valtcho Dintcheff, Adoff Dyker, **Elizabeth Dyker**.

Joso Ecimovic, Gustaf Edwardsson, Hans Eklunz, Johan Ekstrom.

Luigi Finote, Eberhard Fischer.

Nathan Goldsmith, Manoel E. Goncalves, Daniel D. Gronnestad, Alfred Gustafson, Anders Gustafson, Johan Gustafson, Gideon Gustafson.

Aloisia Haas, **Oscar Hadman**, Ingvald O. Hagland, Konrad R. Hagland, Pekko Hakkurainen, **Elin Hakkurainen**, Leon Hampe, **Eluna Hankonen**, Claus Hansen, **Janny Hansen**, Henry Damgavd Hansen, Wendla Heininen, Ignaz Hendekevoic, Jenny Henriksson, **Helga Hervonen, Hildwe Hervonen (child), Laina Hickkinen, Hilda Hillstrom**, John F. A. Holm, Johan Holten, Adolf Humblin.

Ylio Ilieff, Ida Ilmakangas, Pista Ilmakangas, Konio Ivanoff.

Carl Jansen, Jose Netto Jardin, **Carl Jensen**, Hans Peter Jensen, Svenst L. Jensen, Nilho R. Jensen, **Bernt Johannessen, Elias Johannessen**, Nils Johansen, **Oscar Johanson, Oscar L. Johanson**, Erik Johansson, Gustaf Johansson, Jakob A. Johnson, **Alice Johnson, Harold Johnson, Eleanora Johnson (infant)**, Carl Johnsson, Malkolm Johnsson, Lazor Jonkoff, Nielo H.

Jonsson, Katrina Jusila, Mari Jusila, **Erik Jusila**, Henrik Hansen Jutel.

Nikolai Kallio, Johannes H. Kalvig, Milan Karajic, **Einar Karlson**, Nils August Karlson, Tido Kekic, **Anton Kink, Louise Kink, Louise Kink (child)**, Maria Kink, Vincenz Kink, Klas A. Mona Klasen, Mae A. Klasen, Hilda Klasen, Gertrud Klasen (child).

Sofia Laitinen, Kristo Laleff, **Aurora Landegren**, Viktor Larson, Bengt Edvin Larsson, Edvard Larsson, Francis Lefebre, Henry Lefebre (child), Ida Lefebre (child), Ida Lefebre (child), Mathilde Lefebre (child), Antti Leinonen, August Lindablom, Edvard B. Lindell, Elin Lindell, Agda Lindahl, **Einar Lindqvist, Nicola Lulic**, John Lundahl, **Olga Lundin, Jan Lundstripm**.

Fridjof Madsen, Matti Maenpaa, Kalle Makinen, **Leon Mampe**, Dmitri Marinko, Marin Markoff, Philemon Melkebuk, **Guillaume Messemacker, Emma Messemacker, Carl Midtsjo, John Mikanen**, Ivan Misseff, Lazar Minkoff, Dika Mirko, Mito Mitkoff, Sigurd H. Moen, **Albert Moss, Theo Mulder**, Oliver Myhrman.

Penko Naidenoff, Minko Nankoff, Petroff Nedeco, Christo Nenkoff, Manta Nieminen, August F. Nilsson, **Berta Nilson, Helmina Nilson**, Isak Nirva, **Johan Nyoven, Anna Nyston**.

Martin Odahl, Velin Orman, Arthur Olsen, Carl Olsen, Henry Olsen, Ole M. Olsen, Elon Olson, John

Olsson, Elida Olsson, Luka Oreskovic, Maria Oreskovic, Jeko Oreskovic, **Mara Osman**.

Mate Pacruic, Tome Pacruic, Eino Panula, Ernesti Panula, Juho Panula, Maria Panula, Sanni Panula, Urhu Panula (child), William Panula (infant), Jakob Pasic, Petroff Pentcho, Alma C. Paulsson, Gosta Paulsson (child), Paul Paulsson (child) Stina Paulsson (child) Torborg Paulsson (child), Stefo Pavlovic, **E. Pekonemi**, Alfons de Pelsmaker, Nikolai Peltomaki, Ernest Person, Johan Peterson, Ellen Peterson, Matilda Petranec, Olaf Petterson, Vasil Plotcharsky.

Alexander Radeff, Matti Rintamaki, Helene Rosblom, Salf Rosblom (child), Viktor Rosblom, Kristian Rummstvedt.

Carl Salander, **Anna Saljilsvik**, Werner Salonen, **Johan Sandman**, **Agnes Sandstrom**, **Beatrice Sandstrom (child)**, **Margretha Sandstrom (child)**, Todor Sdycoff, **Jean Sheerlinck**, Antti Sihvola, Husen Sivic, **Anna Sjoblom**, Anna Skoog, Carl Skoog (child), Harald Skoog (child), Mabel Skoog (child), Margaret Skoog (child), William Skoog, Petco Slabenoff, Mile Smiljanic, Peter Sohole, Lena Jacobsen Solvang, **Jules Sop**, Ivan Staneff, Mihoff Stoytcho, Ilia Stoyehoff, Ida Strandberg, **Jules Stranden**, Ivan Strilic, Selma Strom (child), Olaf Svensen, Johan Svensson, **Coverin Svensson**, Stanko Syntakoff.

Juho Tikkanen, Lalio Todoroff, **Gunner Tonglin**, Stefan Turcin, **Anna Turgo**, **Hedwig Twekula**.

Jovo Uzelas.

Achille Waelens.

Catharine Van Impe (child), Jacob Van Impe, Rosalie Van Impe, Augusta Vander Van der Planke, Emilie Vander Van der Planke, Jules Vander Van der Planke, Leon Vander Van der Planke, Leo Van der Steen, Joseph Van de Velde, Nestor Van de Walle, Victor Vereruysse, Janko Vook.

Olof Edvin Wende, **August Wennerstrom**, Zinhart Wenzel, Huld A. A. Vestrom, Charles Widegrin, Karl F. Wiklund, Jacob A. Wiklund, Albert Wirz, Camille Wittenrongel.

Renee Zievens, Leo Zimmermann.

PASSENGERS EMBARKED AT CHERBOURG

Marian Assaf, Malake Attala, **Latila Baclini**, **Maria Baclini**, **Eugene Baclini**, **Helene Baclini**, Mohamed Badt, **Ayout Banoura**, Catherine Barbara, Saude Barbara, Tannous Betros, Hanna Boulos, Sultani Boulos, **Nourelain Boulos**, Akar Boulos (child), Elias Banous. Joseph Caram, Maria Caram, Georges Shabini, Emir Farres Chehab, Apostolos Chronopoulos, Demetrios Chronopoulos.

Elias Dibo, Josip Drazenovie, Joseph Elias, **Joseph Elias**, **Leeni Fabini**, **Mustmani Fatma**, Assaf Gerios

Youssef Gerios, Youssef Gerios, Stanio Gheorgheff, Mansour Hanna, Saade Nassr Jean, Markim Johan, **Mary Joseph**, **Franz Karun**, **Anna Karun (child)**, M. Housseing Kassan, Fared Kassem, **Hassef Kassem**, Betros Kalil, **Zahie Khalil**, Thodor Kraeff.

Peter Lemberopoulos, Nicola Malinoff, **Hanna Meme**, Hanna Monbarek, **Omine Moncarek**, **Gonios Moncarek (child)**, **Halim Moncarek (child)**, Mantoura Moussa, **Said Naked**, **Waika Naked**, **Maria Naked**, Mustafa Nasr, **Krikorian Nichan**, **Jamila Nicola**, **Elias Nicola (child)**, **Mansouer Novel**.

Sirayanian Orsen, Zakarian Ortin, **Catherine Joseph Peter**, Mike Peter, Anna Peter, Baccos Rafoul, Razi Raibid, Amin Saad, **Khalil Saad**, Hanna Samaan, Elias Samaan, Youssef Samaan, Mardirosian Sarkis, Lahowd Sarkis, Betros Seman (child), Daher Shedid, Attalla Sleiman, Jovan Stankovic, Thomas Tannous, Daler Tannous, Charles P. Thomas, **Tamin Thomas**, **Assad Thomas (infant)**, John Thomas, Nahli Tonfik, Assad Torfa.

Baulner Useher, **Adele Jane Vagil**, **David Vartunian**, Catavelas Vassilios, Yousif Wazli, Abi Weller, **Ivan Yalsevae**, Antoni Yazbeck, **Salini Yazbeck**, **Brahim Youssef**, Hanne Youssef, **Maria Youssef (child)**, Georges Youssef (child), Tamini Zabour, Hileni Zabour, Maprieder Zakarian.

PASSENGERS EMBARKED AT QUEENSTOWN

Julia Barry, Catherine Bourke, John Bourke, **Bridget Bradley**, **Daniel Buckley**, Katherine Buckley, Jeremiah Burke, Mary Burke, Mary Burns, Mary Canavan, Pat Cannavan, Ellen Carr, Jeannie Car, David Chartens, Patrick Colbert, Thos. H. Conlin, Michel Connaghton, Pat Connors, **Kate Conolly**, Kate Conolly.

Marcella Daly, **Eugene Daly**, **Margaret Devanoy**, Frank Dewan, Patrick Dooley, Elin Doyle, **Bridget Driscoll**, Thomas Emmeth, James Farrell, James Flynn, John Flynn, Joseph Foley, William Foley, Patrick Fox, Martin Gallagher, **Katie Gilnegh**, **Mary Glynn**, Kate Hagardon, Nora Hagarty, Henry Hart, **Nora Healy**, Norah Hemming, Delia Henery, John Horgan.

Annie Jenymin, James Kelly, **Annie K. Kelly**, **Mary Kelly**, Andy Kerane, **John Kennedy**, John Kiernan, Phillip Kiernan, Thomas Kilgannon, Patrick Lane, Denis Lemom, Mary Lemon, Michel Linehan, **Maggie Madigan**, Delia Mahon, **Margareth Mannion**, Mary Mangan, **Katie McCarthy**, **Agnes McCoy**, **Alice McCoy**, **Bernard McCoy**, **Thomas McCormack**, **Delia McDermott**, Michel McElroy, **Mary McGovern**, Katherine McGowan, **Annie McGowan**, Martin McMahon, John Mechan, **Ellie Meeklave**, James Moran, **Bertha Moran**, Daniel J. Morgan, Thomas Morrow, **Katie Mullens**, **Bertha Mulvihill**, **Norah**

Murphy, Mary Murphy, Kate Murphy, Hannah Naughton, Robert Nemagh, Denis O'Brien, Thomas O'Brien, **Hannah O'Brien**, Pat D. O'Connell, Maurice O'Connor, Pat O'Connor, Bert O'Donaghue, **Nellie O'Dwyer, Pat O'Keefe, Norah O'Leary**, Bridget O'Neill, Bridget O'Sullivan.

Katie Peters, Margaret Rice, Albert Rice (child), George Rice (child), Eric Rice (child), Arthur Rice (child) Eugene Rice (child), **Hannah Riordan**, Patrick Ryan, **Edw. Ryan**, Matt Sadlier, James Scanlan, Pat Shaughnesay, **Ellen Shine, Julian Smyth**, Roger Tobin.

CHAPTER 17

THE CREW LIST

The *Titanic* crew list, like its passenger counterpart, is complete but with some discrepencies. It contains the name of at least eight crewmen who were not on board when the *Titanic* struck the iceberg, seven who arrived late and were not let on board and one who deserted before the ship left Ireland. The survivors are in boldface.

DECK CREW

J. Anderson, Ernest Archer, W. Bailey, Joseph Grove Boxhall, F. Bradley, W. Brice, Arthur John Bright, Edward J. Buley, G. Church, Fredrick Clench, G. Clench, F. Couch, Stephen J. Davis, **Alfred Frank Evans,** Frank O. Evans, **Fredrick Fleet, Jack Foley, J. Forward, William French.**

John Hagan, Albert Haines, William Harder, Samuel Ernest Hemmings, Robert Hitchens, George Alfred Hogg, H. Holman, **Robert Hopkins, Albert Edward James Horswell, James S. Humphreys,** John

H. Hutchinson, Archie Jewell, A. Johnson, W. Johnson, **Thomas Jones**, T. W. King, **Reginald Robinson Lee**, L. Leonard, **Charles Herbert Lightoller, Harold Godfrey Lowe, William Lucas**.

William H. Lyons, D. Matherson, M. Mathias, John Maxwell, ? McAuliffe, **W. McCarthy, James McGough**, James Pell Moody, **George Moore**, William McMaster Murdoch, Alfred Nichols, William F. H. O'Loughlin, **Alfred Olliver, Frank Osman**, Sam Parks, **C. H. Pascoe, Walter J. Perkis, W.C. Peters, P. Pigott, Herbert John Pitman, John Poigndestre**.

George Thomas Rowe, R. J. Sawyer, **Joseph Scarrott**, Edward J. Simpson, Edward John Smith, W. Smith, **George Symons**, Fredrick Tamlyn, C. Taylor, Bertram D. Terrell, **W. Turnquist, William R. Weller, Ralph White**, Henry Tingle Wilde, **Walter Wynn**.

ENGINEERING CREW

C. Abraham, R. Adams, **E. Allen**, H. Allen, Alfred S. Alsopp, **J. Avery**, G. W. Bailey, Rich Baines, W. Ball, John Bannon, C. Barlow, Chas. Barnes, J. Barnes, F. W. Barrett, **Fredrick Barrett**, F. Beattie, **George Beauchamp**, Joseph Bell, T. Bendell, G. Bennett, E. Benville, W. Bessant, J. Bevis, C. Biddlecombe, E. Biggs, J. Billows, **Walter Binstead**, A. Black, D. Black, H. Blackman, **P. Blake**, Seaton Blake, T. Blake, J. Blancy, Eustace Blann, W. Bott, P. Bradley, H. Brewer,

W. Brigge, J. Brooks, J. Brown, J. Brown, A. Burroughs, E. Burton, W. Butt.

H. Calderwood, J. Camner, R. Carr, F. Carter, T. Casey, E. Castleman, **George Cavell**, W. Cherrett, G. Chisnall, J. Chorley, **W. Clark**, H. Coe, **John Coffey**, J. Coleman, **Samuel Collins**, **G. Coombes**, H. Cooper, J. Cooper, B. Copperthwaite, D. Corcoran, A. Cotton, J. Couch, **R. Couper**, F.E.G. Coy, H. Crabb, H. Creese, **J. Crimmins**, W. Cross, B. Cunningham, A. Curtis, T. Davies, J. Dawson, **J. Diaper**, W. Dickson, **J. Dilley**, **Thomas Patrick Dillon**, E. C. Dodd, R. Dodd, **F. Doel**, **A. Dore**, F. Doyle, William Duffy, Henry Ryland Dyer, **Frank Dymond**.

A. J. Eagle, C. Eastman, Everett Edward Elliott, George Ervine, W. Evans, W. Farquharson, F. Fay, Auto Ferrary, W. Ferris, **C. W. Fitzpatrick**, H. Fitzpatrick, **E. Flarty**, H. Ford, Thomas Ford, A. Foster, J. Fraser, J. Fraser, **W. Fredricks**, **A. Fryer**, F. Gardner, A. Geer, **G. Godley**, M. W. Golder, J. Gordon, F. Goree, B. Gosling, S. Gosling, **T. Graham**, S. Graves, G. Green, D. Gregory, E. Grodidge, G. Gunnery.

J. Hagan, J. Hall, G. Hallett, B. Hands, G. Hannam, E. Harris, F. Harris, **F. Harris**, N. Harrison, Thomas Hart, Herbert G. Harvey, R. Hasgood, J. Haslin, A. Head, A. Hebb, **Charles Hendrickson**, James H. Hesketh, J. Hill, W. Hinton, C. Hodge, W. Hodges, L. Hodgkinson, R. Hosgood, G. F. Hosking, **Albert S. Hunt**, T. Hunt, C.

J. Hurst, **Walter Hurst**, C. Ingram, T. Instance, John Jacobson, J. Jago, Thos. James, W. Jarvis, N. Joas, **C. Judd**, J. Jukes, Herbert Jupe, **F. Kasper**, C. Kearl, G. Kearl, Jas. Keegan, Jas. Kelly, William Kelly, **George Kemish**, Thos. Kemp, Fredrick Kenchenten, A. Kenzler, T. Kerr, L. Kinsella, J. Kirkham, **T. Knowles.**

T. Lahy, H. Lee, C. Light, W. Light, **W. Lindsay**, W. Lloyd, F. Long, W. Long, W. D. Mackie, W. Magee, **W. Major**, G. Marrett, F. Marsh, L. Maskell, **F. Mason**, J. Mason, A. W. May, Arthur May, W. Mayo, **T. Mayzes**, Thos. McAndrew, W. McAndrews, W. McCastlen, **James McGann**, E. McGarvey, E. McGraw, J. McGregor, T. McInerney, **William McIntyre**, William McQuillan, William McRae, W. McReynolds, Alfred Pirrie Middleton, George Milford, R. Millar, T. Millar, W. Mintram, B. Mitchell, **J. Moore**, R. Moore, R. Moores, A. Morgan, T. Morgan, R. Morrell, A. Morris, W. Morris, **W. Murdoch**.

G. Nettleton, C. Newman, John Noon, J. Norris, B. Noss, **H. Noss, William Nutbean, John O'Connor**, C. Olive, **H. Oliver, C. Othen**, R. Paice, Charles Painter, F. Painter, T. Palles, G. Pand, F. A. Parsons, **J. Pearce, G. Pelham, E. Perry**, H. Perry, G. Phillips, W. Pitfield, **J. Podesta, George Pregnall**, Thomas Preston, **John Priest**, R. Proudfoot, P. Pugh, **Robert Pusey, Thomas Ranger**, J. Read, R. Reed, F. Reeves, **C. Rice**, H. Richards, G. Rickman, G. Roberts, A. Rous, Henry Rudd, C. Sangster, T. Saunders, W. Saunders, W. Saunders, Archibald Scott, **Fred Scott**, A. Self, **E. Self**, **Harry Senior**, Thos. Shea, **F. Sheath**, Jonathan Shepherd, **Alfred Shiers**, C. Shilaber, W. Skeats, P. Sloan, William Small, ? Smith, E. Smith, James M. Smith, H. Smither, G. Snellgrove, W. Snooks, **E. Snow**, **H. Sparkman**, M. Stafford, Augustus Stanbrook, R. Steel, H. Stocker, **A. Street**, H. Stubbs, S. Sullivan.

J. Taylor, **James Taylor**, T. Taylor, **William Henry Taylor**, J. Thomas, **John Thompson**, **Thomas Threlfall**, **G. Thresher**, A. Tizard, F. Toung, J. Tozer, **R. Triggs**, R. Turley, A. Veal, H. Vear, W. Vear, Arthur Ward, J. Ward, F. Wardner, E. Wateridge, W. Watson, S. Webb, F. Webber, Alfred White, Alfred S. White, F. White, William George White, E. Williams, Jack Williams, Bertie Wilson, William Wilton, A. Witcher, F. Witt, H. Witt, H. Woodford, H. Woods, J. Wyeth, Francis Young.

POSTAL CLERKS

William Logan Gwinn, John Starr March, John Richard, Jago Smith, James Bertram Williamson, Oscar S. Woody.

THE BAND

Theodore Brailey, **Roger Bricoux**, **J. Fred C. Clarke**, **Wallace Henry Hartley**, **John Law Hume**, **George Krins**, **Percy C. Taylor**, **J. W. Woodward**.

VICTUALING DEPARTMENT

E. Abbott, P. Ahier, J. Ackerman, A. Ackermann, F. Allan, R. Allan, Baptiste Allaria, E. Allen, F. Allsop, W. Anderson, **Charles E. Andrews**, A. Ashcroft, H. Ashe, G. Aspelagi, E. Ayling, C. Back, **A. Baggott**, E. Bagley, G. Bailey, **Percy Ball**, ? Banfi, A. Barker, E. Barker, Reginald L. Barker, T. Barker, G. Barlow, W. Barnes, A. Barrett, A. Barringer, H. Barrow, W. Barrows, S. Barton, G. Basilico, F. Baxter, H. R. Baxter, L. Bazzi, G. Beedman, William Beere, **Walter Belford**, T. Benhem, **Mrs. Bennett**, B. Bernardi, Florentini Berthold, E. Bessant, E. Best, D. Beux, G. Bietrix, W. Bishop, **Miss Bliss**, J. Blumet, G. Bochet, J. Bochetez, L. Bogie, H. Bolhens, W. Bond, W. Boothby, W. Boston, E. Boughton, **Miss Bowker**, J. Boyd, H. Boyes, J. Bradshaw, G. H. Brewster, **Harold Sydney Bride**, Robert C. Bristow, H. Bristowe, J. Brookman, H. Broom, Athol Broome, **Edward Brown**, W. Brown, H. Buckley, W. Bull, H. Bully, F. Bunmell, **Charles Burgess**, R. Burke, William Burke, E. Burr, **A. Burrage**, Robert Butt, J. Butterworth, J. Byrne.

D. S. Campbell, William Carney, J. Cartwright, C. Casswill, **Miss Caton**, W. Caunt, Herbert Cave, C. Cecil, **J. Chapman**, A. Charboison, John Charman, W.F. Cheverton, G. Chitty, G. Chitty, H. Christmas, T. Clark, A. Coleman, **J. Colgan**, **John Collins**, P. Conway, George Cook, C. Coombs, E. T. Corben, M. Cornaire, A. Coutin, Denton Cox, **F. Crafter, Alfred**

Crawford, H. Crisp, W. Crispin, J. B. Crosbie, Louis Crovelle, **George F. Crowe**, C. Crumplin, **C. Cullen**, **Andrew Cunningham**.

S. Daniels, W. Dashwood, Gordon Davies, J. Davies, R. J. Davies, M. De Breucq, G. Dean, A. Deeble, ? Denison, ? Dennarsico, A. Derrett, P. Deslands, L. Desvernini, J. Dineage, George Dodd, J. Dolby, Italio Donati, F. Donoghue, S. Dornier, W. Doughty, W. Dunford, W. Dyer.

F. Edbrooke, G. B. Ede, F. Edge, C. Edwards, W .H. Egg, **J. Ellis**, W. Ennis, **Henry Samuel Etches**, George Evans, George Evans.

H. Fairall, M. Fanette, E. Farrendon, **William Faulkner**, Carlo Fei, A. Fellows, G. Feltham, F. Fenton, H. Finch, P. W. Fletcher, **W. C. Foley**, E. Ford, F. Ford, W. T. Fox, A. Franklin, Ernest E. S. Freeman, **R. Fropper**.

L. Gatti, R. Geddes, **J.W. Gibbons**, V. Gilardino, J. Giles, P. Gill, S. Gill, **Mrs. Kate Gold**, C. Gollop, A. Goshawk, **Miss Gregson**, G. Claude Gros, Casali Gullio, J. Gunn, **J. Guy**.

R. Halford, F. Hall, S. Halloway, Ernest William Hamblyn, E. Hamilton, A. Harding, **R. Hardwick**, **John Hardy**, C. H. Harris, C.W. Harris, E. Harris, A. Harrison, **John Edward Hart**, **Frederick Hartnell**, H. Hatch, John Hawkesworth, W. Hawksworth, A. Hayter, J. Helnen, E. Hendy, W. Henry, J.

Hensford, T. Hewett, H. Hill, J. Hill, G. Hinckley, G. Hines, S. Hiscock, Leo Hoare, C. Hogg, E. Hogue, T. Holland, F. Hopkins, W. House, A. Howell, H. Hughes, F. Humby, H. Humphreys, J. Hutchinson, **Leo J. Hylands**.

H. Ide, H. Ingrouville, W. Ings, H. Jackson, H. Jaillet, W. Janaway, C. Janin, W. Jeffrey, H. Jenner, C. V. Jenson, **Miss Violet Jessop**, H. Johnson, **James Johnson**, A. Jones, A. Jones, H. Jones, Reginald V. Jones, G. Jouanmault, **Charles Joughin**.

P. Keene, T. Kelland, C. Kennell, W. T. Kerley, H. Ketchley, M. Kieran, James W. Kieran, A. King, Ernest Waldron King, G. King, W. F. Kingscote, A. Kitching, H. Klein, **George Knight**, L. Knight, Bert W. Lacey, W. Lake, A. E. Lane, Andrew J. Latimer, **Miss Lavington**, A. Lawrence, A. Leader, **Mrs. Elizabeth Leather**, G. Lefever, M. Leonard, G. Levett, **Arthur Lewis**, C. Light, **A. Littlejohn**, H. Lloyd, A. Lock, J. Longmiur, J. Lovell, **W. Lucas**, C. Lydiatt.

J. Mabey, **Charles D. MacKay**, G. MacKie, E. Major, R. Mantle, J. Marks, J. W. Marriott, **Miss Marsden, A. Martin, Miss Martin, Mrs. Martin**, A. Mattman, **Paul Mauge, John Maynard**, Alfred Maytum, F. McCarty, T. W. McCawley, Herbert Walter McElroy, James McGrady, **Mrs. McLaren, A. McMicken**, J. McMullen, W. McMurray, A. Mellor, M. V. Middleton, **C. Mills**, A. Mishellany, J. Monoros, J. Monteverdi, A.

Moore, W. Morgan, **F. Morris**, William Moss, T. Mullen, L. Muller.

F. Nannini, **H. Neale**, T. Nicholls, A. Nichols, **W. K. Nichols**.

T. O'Connor, E. R. Olive, W. Orpet, J. Orr, W. Osborne, L. Owens.

R. Pacey, J. Pacherat, J. A. Painton, E. Parsons, R. Parsons, A. Pearce, **Albert Victor Pearcey**, Alex Pedrini, F. Pennell, W. Penny, J. Penrose, L. Perkins, Alfonsi Perotti, W. Perrin, H. Perriton, A. Petrachio, S. Petrachio. Edwin Henry Petty, **Harold Phillimore**, J. Phillips, John George Phillips, L. Piatti, P. Piazza, W. Platt, E. Poggi, R. Pook, **F. Port, Frank M. Prentice**, E. Price, J. A. Prideaux, **H. J. Prior, Mrs. Pritchard**, Chester Proctor, W. Pryce, **Alfred Pugh**, Jno Pusey.

F. Randall, Jas Ranson, E. Ratti, **Frederick Dent Ray**, C. Reed, W. Revall, R. Ricardona, J. R. Rice, P. Rice, Cyril S. Ricks, W. Ridout, A. Rigozzi, F. Roberts, H. Roberts, **Mrs. Roberts**, G. Robertson, J. Robinson, J. Robinson, **Mrs. Annie Robinson**, E. J. Rogers, M. Rogers, R. Ross, Angelo Rotto, P. Rousseau, M. Rowe, **Samuel J. Rule**, G. Rummer, R. Russell, T. Ryan, **W. E. Ryerson**.

G. Sacaggi, Giovenz Salussolia, W. Samuels, D. E. Saunders, **C. J. Savage**, C. Scavino, ? Scott, R. Scovell, Sidney Sedunary, Gino Sesea, W. Sevier, **H. Seward**,

H. Shaw, J. Shea, Sidney Siebert, **A. Simmonds**, F. G. Simmons, W. Simmons, E. Skinner, H. J. Slight, W. Slight, **Miss Mary Sloan**, **Mrs. Maud Slocombe**, J. Smillie, C. Smith, C. Smith, F. Smith, J. Smith, **Miss Smith**, R. G. Smith, Mrs. Snape, J. H. Stagg, **Miss Stap**, S. Stebbing, **John Stewart**, E. Stone, E. Stone, E. A. Stroud, H. Stroud, Jno Strugnell, H. Stubbings, W. Swan, J. Symonds.

George Fredrick Charles Talbot, C. Taylor, L. Taylor, W. Taylor, **F. Terrell**, Ercole Testoni, M. Thayler, **A. Thessinger, A.C. Thomas, B. Thomas**, H. Thompson, W. Thorley, C. Tietz, F. Toms, T. Topp, B. Tucker, G. F. Turner, L. Turner, C. Turvey.

R. Urbini, Ettera Valassori, T. Veal, J. Vicat, P. Vilvarlarge, H. Vine, R. Vioni, H. Voegelin.

S. Wake, Mrs. Wallis, John Walpole, Miss Walsh, E. Ward, P. Ward, **William Ward**, R. Wareham, F. Warwick, W. Watson, T. Weatherstone, Brooke Webb, **August H. Weikman**, W. H. Welch, **Joseph Thomas Wheat, E. Wheelton**, A. White, J. White, L. White, **Thomas Whitely**, A. Whitford, **James Widgery**, A. Williams, **W. Williams**, W. Willis, W. Wiltshire, **J. Windebank, James Witter**, H. Wittman, J. T. Wood, T. Wormald, H. Wrapson, Fredrick Wright, W. Wright.

H. Yearsley, J. Yoshack, L. Zarracchi.

OFFICERS AND RADIO OPERATORS

Captain Edward J. Smith, Purser McElroy, Chief Engineer Fleming, Chief Officer H. T. Wilde, Dr. W.F.N. O'Laughlin, First Officer Murdoch, **Second Officer Lightoller, Third Officer Pitman, Fourth Officer Boxhall, Fifth Officer Lowe**, Sixth Officer Moody, First Wireless Operator John Phillips, **Second Wireless Operator Harold Bride**.

LOOKOUTS
(At Moment of Impact)

Frederick Fleet, Reginald Lee.

CHAPTER 18

THE *TITANIC*'S CARGO MANIFEST

*T*he following goods and services were listed on the *Titanic*'s cargo manifest when it sailed from Southampton. The duplicate listing of some items indicates they were assigned by different companies. The ports of loading were listed as Southampton, Cherbourg, and Queenstown. The port of discharge was listed as New York.

1 case wine, 3 bales of skins, 1 auto, 4 cases of printers blankets, 34 cases of golf clubs, 1 case of toothpaste, 5 cases of drug related sundries, 1 case of brushwire, 8 cases of orchids, 4 cases of pens, 7 cases of cotton, 12 cases of cotton laces, 3 cases of tissues, 4 bales of straw.

4 cases of tulle, 29 cases of cotton, 2 cases of gloves, 1 case of film, 8 cases of bulbs, 28 bags of sticks, 10 boxes of melons, 1 case of china, 1 case of silver goods, 4 cases of straw hats, 1 case of elastic cords, 1 case of

leather, 5 packages of skins, 1 case of skins, 61 cases of tulle, 1 case lace goods, 1 case cotton laces, $^1/_2$ case brushware, 1 case brushware, 3 cases of furniture, 3 cases of silk crape, 2 cases of cotton, 1 case of laces.

4 cases of cottons, 25 cases of biscuits, 42 cases of wines, 7 cases of biscuits, 3 cases of soap perfumes, 5 cases of books, 2 cases of parchments, 2 cases of hardware, 2 cases of books, 2 cases of furniture, 1 case elastics, 1 case gramophone, 4 cases of hoisery, 5 cases of books, 1 case of canvas, 3 cases of prints, 1 case rubber goods.

5 cases of film, 1 case of tweed, 1 case of syringes, a quantity of oak beams, 1 case of plants, 1 speedometer, 8 cases of paste, 4 cases of books, 1 camera and 1 camera stand, 1 case of machinery, 15 cases of alarm apparatus, 4 cases of orchids, 30 cases of plants, 2 cases of lace collars, 2 cases of books, 53 cases of straw, 68 cases of rubber, 10 bags of suspenders, 1 case of cotton, 60 cases of salt powder, 6 cases of soap, 17 packages of wool fat, 1 package of candles, 75 bales of fish, 11 bales of rubber, 5 cases of shells, 1 case of film, 2 cases of hat leather.

2 cases of books, 1 case of woolens, 10 cases of books, 1 bale of skins, 1 crate of machinery, 1 case of printed matter, 386 rolls of linoleum, 437 casks of tea, 4 bales of skins, 134 cases of rubber, 76 cases of dragon's blood, 2 cases of gum, 3 cases of books, 95 cases of

books, 117 cases of sponges, 12 packages of periodicals, 3 cases of woolens, 53 cases of champagne, 1 case of felt, 8 dozen tennis balls, 1 dozen engine packings, 1 case surgical goods, 1 case ironware, 4 cases printed matter, 1 case of cloth, 4 cases of printed matter, 1 case cloth, 4 cases printed matter, 1 case of machinery, 1 case of books, 1 dozen notions, 1 case of elastics, 2 cases of books, 1 box of golf balls, 5 cases of instruments, 4 rolls of lineoleum, 1 case of hats.

3 bales of leather, 5 cases of books, 6 cases of confectionery, 1 case of tin tubes, 2 cases of soap, 2 cases of boots, 3 cases of books, 2 cases of furniture, 1 case of pamphlets, 1 dozen paints, 1 case of eggs, 1 dozen cases of whiskey, 10 packages of periodicals, 1 case iron jacks, 1 dozen bulbs, 1 case of hosiery, 1 case of clothing, 8 cases of hairnets, 1 case of

silk goods, 1 case of tissues, 1 case of hairnets, 1 case of silk goods, 2 cases of silk goods, 3 cases of silk goods, 1 case of gloves, 30 packages of tea, 2 cases of books, 5 cases of books, 1 bag of frames.

1 case of cotton, 2 cases of stationery, 1 case of scientific instruments, 1 case of sundries, 3 cases of test cord, 1 case of briar pipes, 1 case of sundries, 2 cases of printed matter, 1,196 bags of potatoes, 318 bags of potatoes, 1 case of velvets, 18 bales of straw goods, 1 case of raw feathers, 2 cases of linens, 3 cases of tissue, 3 cases of rabbit skins, 1 case of auto parts, 1 case

of feathers, 3 cases of leather, 15 cases of rabbit hair, 11 cases of feathers, 1 case of tissue, 11 cases of refrigerating machinery, 18 cases of machinery, 1 case of packed packages.

3 cases of tissue, 2 barrels of mercury, 1 barrel of earth, 2 barrels of glassware, 3 cases of printed matter, 1 case of straw braids, 1 case of straw hats, 1 case of cheese, 3 cases of hosiery, 3 cases of silk goods, 1 case of brushware, 2 cases of ribbons, 2 cases of flowers, 1 case of gloves, 6 bales of cork, 75 cases of anchovies, 1 case of liquor, 225 cases of mustard, 190 cases of liquor, 25 cases of syrup, 25 cases of preserves, 12 cases of butter, 18 cases of oil, 2 hogsheads of vinegar, 6 cases of preserves, 19 cases of vinegar, 8 cases of dry fruit, 16 hogsheads of wine, 185 cases of wine, 110 cases of brandy, 10 hogsheads of wine, 15 cases of cognac, 100 cases of shelled walnuts.

70 bundles of cheese, 20 bundles of cheese, 2 cases of cognac, 1 case of liquor, 38 cases of oil, 107 cases of mushrooms, 1 case of pamphlets, 25 cases of sardines, 8 cases of preserves, 50 cases of wine, 6 casks of vermouth, 4 cases of wine, 11 cases of shelled walnuts, 100 bales of shelled walnuts, 300 cases of shelled walnuts, 35 bags of rough wood, 50 bundles of cheese, 5 bundles of cheese, 50 bundles of cheese.

190 bundles of cheese, 50 bundles of cheese, 10 bundles of cheese, 50 bundles of cheese, 30 bundles of

cheese, 30 bundles of cheese, 10 bundles of cheese, 15 bundles of cheese, 41 cases of filter paper, 22 cases of mushrooms, 15 cases of peas, 10 cases of mixed vegetables, 25 cases of olives, 12 bundles of capers, 10 cases of fish, 25 cases of olive oil, 14 cases of mushrooms.

SUGGESTED READING

The flood of *Titanic* books began almost immediately. Within a month of the disaster, a half dozen titles, totaling an estimated 400,000 copies, were being sold in stores and hawked by door-to-door salesmen. When they had sold all the copies they possibly could, enterprising but not too ethical publishers put a new cover on the same books and sold them again.

For the record, the first book out on the *Titanic* was called *The Sinking of the Titanic and Great Sea Disasters*. Over the years, the *Titanic* has continued to grip the imagination, and publishers have rolled out countless volumes on every conceivable aspect of the tragedy.

What follows is a selection of recommended books.

Anderson, Roy. *White Star.* Prescot, UK: T. Stephenson & Sons, 1964.

Archibold, Rick and Dana McCauley. *Last Dinner on the Titanic: Menus and Recipes From the Legendary Liner.* NY: Hyperion, 1997.

Baker, W.J. *A History of the Marconi Company.* London: Metheun, 1970.

Ballard, Robert and Rick Archibold. *The Discovery of the Titanic.* NY: Warner Books, 1987.

Beesley, Lawrence. *The Loss of the SS Titanic: Its Story and Its Lessons.* Boston: Houghlin Mifflin, 1912.

Behe, George. *Titanic: Psychic Forewarnings of a Tragedy.* Wellingborough, UK: Patrick Stephens, 1988.

Biel, Steven. *Down With the Old Canoe: A Cultural History of the Titanic Disaster.* NY: Norton,1996.

Bonsall, Thomas E. *Titanic.* NY: Gallery Books, 1987.

Booth, John and Sean Coughlan. *Titanic: Signals of Disaster.* White Star Publications, 1993.

Boyd-Smith, Peter. *Titanic from Rare Historical Reports.* Southhampton, UK: Steamship Publications, 1994.

Brinnen, John Malcolm. *The Sway of the Grand Saloon.* NY: Delacorte, 1961.

Brown, Alexander Crosby. *Women and Children Last: The Loss of the Steamship Arctic.* NY: G.P. Putnam, 1961.

Brown, Rustie. *The Titanic, the Psychic and the Sea.* Lomita, CA: Blue Harbor Press, 1981.

Bryceson, Dave. *The Titanic Disaster: As Reported in the British National Press April-July 1912.* NY: Norton, 1997.

Bullock, Shaun F. *A Titanic Hero: Thomas Andrews, Shipbuilder 1973–1912.* Riverside, CT: 7C's Press, 1973.

Cooper, Gary. *The Man Who Sank the Titanic? The Life and Times of Captain Edward J. Smith.* Witan, 1992.

Cronin, Anthony. *R.M.S. Titanic.* Dublin: Raven Arts Press, 1981.

Davie, Michael. *Titanic: The Death And Life of a Legend.* NY: Knopf, 1987.

Dodge, Washington. *The Loss of the Titanic.* Riverside, CT: 7C's Press, 1912.

Eaton, John. P. and Charles A. Haas. *Titanic: Destination Disaster—The Legends and the Reality.*. NY: Norton, 1996.

Eaton, John P. and Charles A. Haas. *Titanic: Triumph and Tragedy.* NY: Norton, 1995.

Everett, Marshal. *Wreck and Sinking of the Titanic.* NY: L.H. Walter, 1912.

Gardiner, Robin and Dan van der Vat. *The Riddle of the Titanic.* London: Weidenfeld and Nicolson, 1995.

Garrett, Richard. *Atlantic Disaster: Titanic and Other Victims of the North Atlantic.* London: Buchan & Enright, 1986.

Gracie, Archibald. *The Truth About the Titanic.* NY: M. Kennerley, 1913.

Harrison, Leslie. *A Titanic Myth: The Californian Incident.* London: William Kimber, 1986.

Harrison, Leslie. *Defending Captain Lord: A Titanic Myth: Part Two.* Images Publications, 1996.

Heyer, Paul. *Titanic Legacy: Disaster as Media Event*

and Myth. Westport, CT: Praeger, 1995.

Hilton, George W. Eastland: *Legacy of the Titanic.* Stanford, CA: Stanford UP, 1995.

Hoffman, William and Jack Grimm. *Beyond Reach: The Search for the Titanic.* NY: Beaufort Books, 1982.

Hyslop, Donald, Alastair Forsyth, and Sheila Jemima, eds. *Titanic Voices: Memories From the Fateful Voyage.* NY: St. Martin's Press, 1997.

Jessop, Violet and John Maxwell Graham. *The Newly Discovered Memoirs of Violet Jessop Who Survived Both the Titanic and Britannic Disasters.* Dobbs Ferry, NY: Sheridan House, 1997.

Lightoller, Charles H. *Titanic And Other Ships.* London: Nicholson & Watson, 1935.

Lord, Walter. *The Night Lives On.* NY: Morrow, 1986.

Lord, Walter. *A Night to Remember.* NY: Bantam, 1991.

Lynch, Donald and Ken Marschall. *Titanic: An Illustrated History.* NY: Hyperion, 1992.

MacInnis, Joseph. *Titanic: In a New Light.* Charlottesville, VA: Thomasson-Grant, 1992.

Marcus, Geoffrey Jules. *The Maiden Voyage.* NY: Viking, 1969.

Mowbray, Jay H. *Sinking of the Titanic.* NY: G.W. Bertron, 1912.

Padfield, Peter. *The Titanic and the Californian.* NY: John Day, 1966.

Pellegrino, Charles R. *Her Name, Titanic: The Untold Story of the Sinking and Finding of the*

Unsinkable Ship. NY: McGraw-Hill, 1988.

Pellow, James and Dorothy Kendle. *A Lifetime on the Titanic: The Biography of Edith Haisman*. London: Island Books, 1995.

Quinn, Paul J. *Titanic at Two A.M.: An Illustrated Narrative With Survivor Accounts*. Fantail, 1997.

Reade, Leslie. *The Ship That Stood Still: The Californian and Her Mysterious Role in the Titanic Disaster*. NY: Norton, 1993.

Stenson, Patrick. *The Odyssey of C. H. Lightoller*. NY: Norton, 1984.

Thayer, John B. *The Sinking of the Titanic*. Conn: 7C's Press, 1984.

Tyler, Sidney. *A Rainbow of Time and Space: Orphans of the Titanic*. Tucson, AZ: Aztek Corp., 1981.

Wade, Wyn Craig. *Titanic: End of a Dream*. NY: Penguin, 1992.

Wels, Susan. *Titanic: Legacy of the World's Greatest Ocean Liner*. NY: Time-Life, 1997.

Winocour, Jack. *The Story of the Titanic: As Told by Its Survivors*. NY: Dover, 1960.

TITANIC FICTION

Bainbridge, Beryl. *Every Man for Himself*. NY: Carroll & Graf, 1996.

Bass, Cynthia. *Maiden Voyage*. NY: Villard, 1996.

Clarke, Arthur C. *The Ghost from the Grand Banks*. NY: Bantam, 1990.

Cussler, Clive. *Raise the Titanic!* NY: Viking, 1976.

Finney, Jack. *From Time to Time.* NY: Simon & Schuster, 1995.

Gardner, Martin, ed. *The Wreck of the Titanic Foretold?* Buffalo, NY: Prometheus, 1997.

Hansen, Erik Fosner and Joan Tate, trans. *Psalm at Journey's End.* NY: Farrar, Straus & Giroux, 1996.

Jarvis, Charles E. *Titanic Interlude: A Novel.* Lowell, MA: Ithaca, 1982.

Robertson, Morgan. *Futility: Or the Wreck of the Titan.* Buccaneer Books, 1991.

Seil, William. *Sherlock Holmes and the Titanic Tragedy: A Case to Remember.* London: Breese, 1996.

Stanwood, Donald. *The Memory of Eva Ryker.* NY: Coward, McCann and Geoghegan, 1978.

Steel, Danielle. *No Greater Love.* NY: Delacorte, 1991.

TITANIC POETRY

Ball, Richard. *The Last Voyage of the Titanic.* Corsham, UK: Gazebo Books, 1968.

Cronin, Anthony. *R.M.S. Titanic.* Dublin: Raen Arts Press, 1981.

Dixon, J. Qallan. *Wreck of the Steamship Titanic.* Buffalo, NY: Sovereign, 1912.

Drew, Edwin. *The Wreck of the Titanic: Treated in Verse.* London: W. Nicholson & Sons, 1912.

Greeley, Horace. *The Wreck of the Titanic: A Poem.* Brooklyn: Donald Sinclair.

Howell, J. A. *The Great Ship Titanic and Its Disaster.*

Ridgewood, W.VA: Yew Pine Independent, 1913.

MacFie, Ronald Campbell. *The Titanic: An Ode of Immortality.* London: E. MacDonald, 1912.

Pratt, E. J. *The Titanic.* Toronto: MacMillan, 1935.

Root, E. Merrill. *Of Perilous Seas.* Francistown, NH: Golden Quill Press, 1964.

Stahl, C. Victor. *The Sinking of The Titanic and Other Poems.* Boston: Sherman French, 1915.

TITANIC MUSICALS AND DRAMA

Campion, Narcissa and Sam Abel. *The Great American Disaster Musical, or The Titanic Goes Hawaiian.* Dover, MA: Charles River Creative Arts Press, 1984. (musical)

Durang, Christopher. *Titanic.* NY: Dramatists Play Service, 1983. (drama)

Hatcher, Jeffrey. *Scotland Road.* NY: Dramatists Play Service, 1996. (drama)

Polistina, Anthony and Joe DaVersa. *Titanic: A Musical Telling.* Songrise Music, 1996. (musical)

Siebert, Wilhelm Dieter. *Untergang der Titanic.* Berlin: Bote & Bock, 1984. (operatic libretto)

Yeston, Maury and Peter Stone. *Titanic.* Opened Lunt-Fontanne Theatre, New York City, April 23, 1997. (musical)

ARTICLES OF INTEREST

Ballard, Robert D. "How We Found *Titanic.*" *National Geographic,* December 1985.

Ballard, Robert D. "A Long, Last Look at *Titanic*." *National Geographic,* December 1986.

Brownlee, Shannon. "Explorers of Dark Frontiers." *Discover*, February 1986.

Colligan, Doug and Charles R. Pellegrino. "*Titanic* Robots." *Omni*, July 1986.

Culliton, Barbara J. "Woods Hole Mulls *Titanic* Expedition." *Science*, August 26, 1977.

Collyer, Charlotte. "How I Was Saved From the *Titanic*." *Washington Post,* May 26, 1912.

"The Deathless Story of the Titanic." *Lloyds Weekly News,* 1985.

Dudley, Brian A. "The Construction of the *Titanic*." *Steamboat Bill,* Spring 1972.

Duff Gordon, Lady Cosmo. "I Was Saved From the *Titanic*." *Coronet*, June 1951.

Kennedy, C. and S. Prentice. "A Night Still Remembered: Checking In with a Last Survivor." *MacCleans,* January 23, 1978.

Lightoller, Charles H. "Testimonies From the Field." *Christian Science Journal,* October, 1912.

Lord, Walter. "Maiden Voyage." *American Heritage,* December, 1955.

"The Olympic and the Titanic." *Scientific American,* June 17, 1911.

"*Olympic* and *Titanic*." *The Shipbuilder,* Summer, 1911, reprinted by Patrick Stephens Ltd.

Rostron, Arthur H. "The Rescue of the *Titanic* Survivors." *Scribner's Monthly,* March, 1913.

"Titanic." *Oceanus*. Winter, 1985.

Tucker, Jonathan B. "Robot Subs." *High Technology,* February, 1986.

"The White Star Liners *Olympic* and *Titanic.*" *The Engineer,* March 4, 1910.

"The White Star Liner Titanic." *Engineering*, May 26, 1911.

Woods, W .J. "Construction of the *Titanic.*" *Marine Review,* May, 1912.

Young, Filson. "God and Titan." *Saturday Review,* April 20, 1912.

SUGGESTED VIEWING

The discovery of the *Titanic's* resting place has been a boon to the documentary film-making industry. A number of videos focusing on the sinking of the *Titanic* and the subsequent expeditions by Robert Ballard are available. These are the best of the bunch.

The Secrets of the Titanic, National Geographic Video, 1986. Chronicles the last days of the *Titanic*, its final resting place and the Robert Ballard expeditions that rediscovered the ship 73 years later. Narrated by Martin Sheen.

Return to the Titanic. 1988. Television special. A documentary covering the French expedition headed by George Tulloch to the *Titanic* site and the recovery of artifacts. Hosted by Telly Savalas

Titanic: Treasures of the Deep. 1992. Originally a CBS television special, this documentary covers the joint Canadian, Russian, and American expedition. Narrated by Walter Cronkite.

Titanic: The Nightmare and the Dream, 1986. Television special.

Titanic: A Question of Murder, 1987. Television special.

Memories of the Titanic, 1991. Eleven survivors recall the tragedy.

Titanica, IMAX, 1992. The first Ballard expedition.

Explorers of the Titanic, 1995. Television video.

Titanica 1995. IMAX.

SUGGESTED WEBSITES

*T*he Internet is an endless highway of knowledge, facts, and obscura regarding the *Titanic*. Some of the most helpful websites in this *Titanic* search are:

The Official *Titanic* Movie Site—
    http://www.titanicmovie.com
Britannica Online—http://www.eb.com
Tribute To Author Walter Lord—
    http://www2.wco.com/~wseright/walterlord
Molly Brown House Museum—
    http://www.mollybrown.com
Robert Ballard's Jason Project—
    http://www.jasonproject.org/expedition.html
Virginia Newspaper Project—
    http://www.lib.virginia.edu/cataloging/vnp/titanic/
    titanic1.html
Nic Wilson's *Titanic*, *Olympic* and *Britannic* Page—
    http://www.powerup.com.au/~nicw/index.htm
Astronomy and Trivia at Unsinkable RMS *Titanic*—
    http://www.geocities.com/CapeCanaveral/Hangar/
    7574/titanic.htm

Discovery Channel Online—
http://www.discovery.com/area/science/titanic/tita
nicopener.html
Titanic Historical Society—
http://www2.titanic1.org/titanic1
Titanic Information Site—
http://www.netins.net/showcase/js/titanic
Andrew's Report on the *Titanic*—
http://members.aol.com/April1912/index.html
Dave's Titanic Page —
http://www.angelfire.com/ny/titanicpage/
Encyclopedia Smithsonian: The *Titanic*—
http://www.si.edu/resource/faq/nmah/titanic.htm
Gary's Titanic Page—
http://www.ilap.com/~garnold/titanic.htm
In Memoriam: RMS *Titanic*—
http://www.wwa.com/~dsp/titanic
Jim's Titanic Site—
http://www.intercall.net/~jsadur/titanic/
Ocean Planet: How Deep Can They Go?—
http://www.seawifs.gsfc.nasa.gov/Ocean_Planet/
HTML/titanic.html
Original Titanic Page—
http://www.cport.k12.ky.us/ffhs/Curriculum/
History/TITANIC/Titanic.htm
Ravensworld Titanic Page—
http://www.ravens.net/titanic/index.html
RMS *Titanic* and Her Sisters—
http://www.powerup.com.au/~nicw/index.htm

RMS *Titanic*: Her Passengers and Crew—
http://www.rnplc.co.uk/eduweb/sites/phind
Titanic and Other White Star Ships—
http://members.aol.com/MNichol/Titanic.index.html
Titanic Diagram—http://members.aol.com/lorbus
Titanic Society of South Africa—
http://www.onwe.co.za/titanic

ACKNOWLEDGMENTS

*I*t is not often that one has the chance to step back in time. Researching *Total Titanic: The Most Up-to-Date Guide to the Diaster of the Century* afforded me that opportunity and, in the process, the chance to look over the shoulders of some dedicated and quite thorough journalists and historians.

First of all I would like to thank Edward Kamuda, president and founding member of the *Titanic* Historical Society, who was kind enough to delay his morning rounds at the *Titanic* Historical Society Museum to fill me in on his organization and to offer some insights into the exploitation that quickly followed on the heels of the sinking of the *Titanic*.

There were books aplenty to help set the record straight, but particular kudos go to Walter Lord's classic and quite human investigation, *A Night to Remember*. Lord juggles the cold, hard facts of the disaster with its human drama, revealing the frailty and triumph of the human spirit. Ever the thorough investigator, Lord came back to the well years later with *The Night Lives On*, a book that pointed out the facts while dispelling the myths and legends.

Charles Pellegrino took an equally effective approach in his book *Her Name, Titanic*, leapfrogging, in a close to surrealist manner, between the story of the *Titanic* and the effort, years later, of Dr. Robert Ballard and his crew of scientists and explorers to bring the *Titanic* and its secrets back into the light.

Other books that tell intriguing elements of the story include *Lost Films*, by Frank Thompson; *The Story of the Titanic As Told by Its Survivors*, by Jack Winocour; and *Titanic: An Illustrated History*, by Don Lynch, Ken Marschall, and Robert D. Ballard.

Barbara Barker, thanks for letting me borrow your books.

And finally a special heartfelt thanks to my wife Nancy and my daughter Rachael. They shared the pressures and the writer tantrums. We lived to tell this tale. Love to you.

—Marc Shapiro